HER WEREWOLF DEFENDER

WEREWOLF GUARDIAN ROMANCE SERIES

JODI VAUGHN

NEWSLETTER SIGN UP

CHAPTER 1

*J*ust outside of Little Rock, Arkansas
Present Day

"PENISES ARE LIKE SHOES. They come in all shapes and sizes. When you find the right one, no matter how hard you try, you will never wear it out."

Jayden Parker stumbled to a halt as the unmistakable sound of Granny's voice came from the other side of the living room door.

He closed his eyes, fought back a shiver and whispered a silent prayer that Granny wasn't actually talking to someone.

"Please let her be reading *Cosmo* out loud." The magazine was like her morning devotional. She had this bad habit of sharing the sage advice she found in the magazine with him whenever he came over for breakfast. When she'd read the article about oral sex, Jayden had almost tossed his eggs and bacon on the tile floor.

1

He scrubbed his hand over his face as his gut twisted in anticipation.

He shouldn't have come. He should have created another excuse for why he wasn't visiting her as much as he once did. He tried to play it off by telling her he was busy with his new job as a Guardian for the Arkansas Werewolves. He'd always say he was on some new mission or some other bullshit answer to keep her from complaining so much.

Usually she bought it, but now, not so much.

JAYDEN OPENED his eyes and steadied himself. Before he could change his mind and escape out the door, he sucked in a breath and turned the corner, forcing his feet to carry him into the living room. The scent of cinnamon and sugar hung heavy in the air. Maybe Granny had baked his favorite cookies in an attempt to bribe him into visiting more often.

The second he stepped into the living room he froze. About twenty women of all ages were crowded into Granny's tiny living room. Some were perched on the couch and chairs, while other sat on the floor. There wasn't even enough room for him to walk through to get to the kitchen.

Granny stood at the front of the room like a gray-haired Vanna White holding a neon green dildo in her hand.

"I'm in hell," Jayden murmured under his breath as his stomach turned.

When Granny had started selling sex toys in Louisiana as a way to make some extra income, he'd tried his best to talk her out of it. But she was a persistent old goat, and he had stopped nagging her about it. He figured that no one would be interested in some old woman peddling that merchandise, and she would eventually give it up.

What he didn't take into account was Granny's tenacity. When she got something in her head she didn't give up. And in less than a year she was pulling in a six-figure salary. She was like a dog with a bone, refusing to give up her status as a self-made entrepreneur. Now, after their recent move to Arkansas for his newly acquired job as a Guardian, he had hoped that Granny would give up her sex toy industry in an attempt to fit into the conservative state.

Boy, was he wrong.

He'd needed a fresh start, and Arkansas had offered him an opportunity. Louisiana held too many bad memories.

A few months ago, Jayden had helped Arkansas werewolf and friend, Damon Trahan, find a kidnapped college girl. That led to Jayden ending up on the wrong side of a pack of rogue red werewolves. What happened that night had been worse than the bruises and broken bones his Granny could see. Because of his werewolf blood, those injuries had healed. But some scars he carried went deeper. Way deeper. Those were the things he could never tell his Granny, or anyone for that matter, despite how hard she tried to get him to talk to her.

Since then, Granny had been watching him, looking at him like she could see what was rolling around in his head. The last fucking thing he needed was his Granny seeing how fucked up his brain had gotten from his one night of torture.

He eased back a step, hoping to escape out the front door before Granny saw him. He made a quick turn just as his foot caught the corner of the rug. He stumbled and his hip bumped the corner of the sofa table, rattling the ruby red bowl that held decorative colorful glass balls.

Granny turned. A smile stretched her weathered face. "Jayden. I didn't hear you come in." She waded towards him through the puddle of people on the floor.

"I didn't know you were having a party. I can come back later." Jayden smiled tightly and turned to go.

Granny latched onto his arm, her smile growing wider.

She turned and faced the room. "Everyone, I'd like you to meet my grandson, Jayden. He's single, you know."

Jayden gritted his teeth and wrestled his smile into place as a collective giggle went up in the room. The last thing he needed was a date. Hell, he could get a piece of ass anytime, anywhere. It was just lately, since that night in Louisiana, he really hadn't felt the urge to be with a female. Maybe he was too fucked up to be fixed.

Jayden gently pried Granny's hands off his bicep. "I didn't mean to interrupt your little … sex party." Boy, did those words not want to come out.

"Now was that so hard so say?" Granny rolled her eyes and faced the room.

"You have no idea." Jayden ran his hand across the back of his neck. Laugher erupted in the room and he flashed them all an apologetic smile. From the corner of his eye, someone caught his attention, causing him to do a double-take.

It was her. Haley Guthrie. The girl he'd rescued in Louisiana. What the hell was she doing here?

The hair on the back of his neck stood at attention. He would know her by her scent alone, even if he weren't looking dead at her. His gaze lingered a few seconds too long before he forced himself to look away.

Granny must have followed his gaze, the eagle-eyed detective that she was, since the next words that came out of her mouth were directed at him.

"You remember Haley, don't you?" Granny smiled as she glanced at her.

"Of course." Jayden flashed Haley a polite smile, though his gut felt like ice. "I'm surprised to see you here. I thought you would be busy with your classes at LSU."

Haley blushed as she squirmed in her seat on the floor.

"Oh, she transferred to University of Arkansas. She's just

4

here visiting for the weekend," Granny offered before Haley could open her mouth.

Haley quickly averted her gaze. It was obvious that she was trying her hardest to look anywhere but at him. She didn't want to be reminded of that night either.

Did he blame her? No. Did it still hurt him to know he'd failed her? Hell, yes.

"Well, I really have to get going. I've got a meeting in"—Jayden glanced at his Luminox watch—"about ten minutes." He kissed Granny's wrinkled cheek and gave the women a wave, his gaze effectively floating over Haley as he made his way to the kitchen. Since he was here he might as well grab a couple of cookies on his way out since he'd missed both breakfast and lunch.

Jayden snagged a handful of snickerdoodles and had his hand on the knob of the back door by the time Granny caught up to him.

"Will you be back for dinner? I was going to make pot roast." Her hopeful voice made him feel lower than dog shit.

Jayden plastered that fucking smile on his face and glanced over his shoulder. "I'm not sure. It sounded like this meeting with Barrett may take a while. I'll let you know." He snatched opened the door and hurried out into the brilliant sunshine of the spring day. The breeze ruffled his hair as he hurried to his Harley Davidson Breakout. He took a bite of his cookie as he contemplated why Haley Guthrie was here. His stomach clenched and he quickly lost his appetite. He tossed the remaining cookies to the ground before straddling his motorcycle.

With Haley now living in Arkansas, Jayden was certain of one thing.

His hellish past he'd thought he left behind in Louisiana had just followed him straight to Arkansas.

"HALEY, YOU LIED." Dana, her college roommate shot her a frown and playfully elbowed her in the side. Dana's dark brown hair cascaded over her shoulders as her caramel brown eyes twinkled with amusement. "You said you didn't know anyone in Arkansas."

Haley swallowed and avoided her friend's gaze. "I didn't know Jayden lived in Arkansas. I only met him once and that was in Louisiana." She shrugged and buried her nose in the catalogue of sex toys, hoping Dana would drop the subject of Jayden Parker. Jayden was one topic she didn't want to discuss. Not with anyone. Judging by the glare he'd shot her, he didn't want to be anywhere near her. She'd caused him enough pain for a lifetime.

She should have never come with Dana, but she needed help and was out of options. Coming to the sex party gave her an excuse to visit the compound where the Pack Master of Arkansas lived.

It had been over almost five months since her parents had forced her to transfer colleges. She had spent those five months going from classes to her room, functioning on a basic level of eating, sleeping, and studying.

Haley Guthrie had gone from being the apple of her parents' eyes to dog shit on the bottom of their expensive shoes, in the matter of a single night. Her kidnapping had changed the course of her life forever.

It was startling to her that the people who raised her, who spoiled her, and bragged on her, could change their affection at the drop of a dime. It was only after she'd been rescued and brought home that she discovered that her parents' love was conditional and shallow. She expected them to rejoice in her safe return home, but what she got was disappointment that she had brought shame upon their family name.

"Damn, girl, Jayden is fine. I heard he's built like a stallion, if you know what I mean." Dana waggled her eyebrows as she passed Haley an enormous red dildo.

"I wouldn't know." Haley's heart beat loudly in her ears and she quickly passed the obscene toy to the woman sitting next to her. Sex was the last thing on her mind. She really didn't see the appeal of all these plastic gadgets and candy-flavored underwear. It wasn't like she was in a relationship. Not anymore.

"You need to start dating again." Dana's brow furrowed as she turned on the spinning dildo shaped like a sea lion. "Your last relationship was what? Four months ago?"

"Five." Five months, two weeks, and three days. The night she was kidnapped, a pack of rogue red wolves said they needed to repopulate their scarce numbers. And they wanted her to be their sex slave. Lucky her. It was the night her boyfriend and her parents had deemed her damaged goods. After all, who would want to mate her now, right? She came from a wealthy werewolf family and reputation meant everything.

"I don't think I'm ready." Haley pretended to read the ingredients of a cherry-flavored lubricant. No way in hell was she ready to date right now, and it didn't have anything to do with a broken heart.

A few weeks after moving into the dorms, Haley started receiving handwritten notes under her door once a week. They had started innocently enough with things like, *"Hello pretty girl"* and *"You blind the sun with your smile."* At first Haley had thought they were meant for Dana.

But then she began receiving them every day and the messages had been more personal, more intense. Whoever left them made sure to write Haley's name on the outside so there would be no mistaking who they were intended for.

"I see how the all the guys look at you, Haley. You could

have any hot guy on campus." Dana shook her head. "Hell, if I were single and looked like you I'd be exercising my options."

"Whatever. I can't imagine you and Mark not together. You guys look like the perfect couple, Ken and Barbie." Haley smiled.

"Yeah, but it gets a little boring. He's always studying and striving to keep his four point oh. This leaves very little time for me." Dana pouted.

"Well, order this little number. " Haley pointed to a red lace teddy that hardly covered anything. "I'm sure he'll make time for you then."

"Oh, I like that one." Dana scribbled the item number in her order form and cut her eyes to Haley. "Shall I put you down for something? A vibrator, maybe? It could be an early Christmas gift."

"No, thanks." Haley scowled and glanced at the empty doorway. The minute Jayden had locked eyes on her, she'd struggled to remain sitting. All she wanted to do was get up and go after him. She still hadn't had the opportunity to thank him for what he had done for her that night in Louisiana. If Jayden hadn't shown up, she would have ended up being repeatedly raped and eventually killed. A shiver ran down her back as she wrapped her arms around herself.

She tried to tell herself that was the only reason she wanted to go after him. That she didn't feel anything other than gratitude for the male who'd risked everything to save her.

She'd seen how his eyes iced over when they landed on her. Though he covered easily and managed to hide it from everyone else in the room, Haley knew that Jayden was not pleased to see her there. Apparently this was his town and his state now, and he didn't approve of sharing that territory. She was as offensive to him as she was to her parents.

"It doesn't matter," she said softly, swallowing back the bitterness rising from her chest

"What doesn't matter?" Dana didn't look up from her catalogue.

Haley chuckled nervously, not realizing she had actually spoken out loud. Damn, she needed to stop doing that. It was a habit her parents hated and she had made an effort to not do it. But since they distanced themselves from their only daughter, she'd not really cared who she pleased. Not anymore. She was going to make only one person happy. And that was herself.

Haley opened up her catalogue with a renewed interest. No time like the present.

"It doesn't matter which one. Just pick me out one. But I'm buying it. I'm sure you're going to break the bank ordering all those edible panties for your guy to enjoy."

GRANNY WATCHED WITH A HEAVY HEART, as Jayden tore down the street on his new gray Harley Davidson motorcycle. Since they'd moved to Arkansas, he didn't drive his Mustang much anymore. These days he always seemed to prefer riding his motorcycle on every mission that Barrett sent him to. But that wasn't what worried her.

Jayden was working too much. She could see the strain in his eyes when he walked into the room. Usually when there were women around, Jayden hung around and flirted. He'd always had his share of admirers growing up. That was no different now. At the age of thirty Jayden was as handsome as ever. And she wanted him to finally settle down with a mate of his own. But since that one night in Louisiana something about him had changed. Though he tried to hide it, she still saw. He was different now, harder.

Life was too short to live with regrets and pain from the

past. This she knew. But she wasn't sure that this time she would be the one to help her grandson heal.

Jayden walked into the gray concrete building that housed the training facilities of the Arkansas Werewolf Guardians. The building also housed the office of his, "don't fuck with me" Pack Master, Barrett Middleton.

He'd met Barrett years ago when he'd asked him to find some Intel on a werewolf who was suspected of dealing meth down in Louisiana. After he provided the info to the Arkansas Pack Master, Barrett had continued to call on Jayden throughout the years whenever they needed some Intel. They usually spoke through a third party, up until a few months ago when Arkansas Were female, Ava Renfroe, had been kidnapped by the same rogue wolves that had taken Haley. Jayden had been called upon by his childhood friend Damon Trahan to help. After both women had been rescued, Barrett had offered him an official position with the Arkansas Pack. Jayden welcomed the opportunity to get away and make a fresh start. He didn't need any reminders of what had happened that night in Louisiana. Maybe with a change of scenery he could get his head right. Until he had spotted the beautiful blonde-haired blue-eyed Haley Guthrie sitting in his Granny's living room.

"Maybe I'm not supposed to get a fresh start. Maybe I'm going to have to deal with this shit for the rest of my life." Jayden plowed his fist into the cinderblock wall. The sting bit into his knuckle for a brief second before the healing proper-ties in his blood regenerated the bruised flesh.

"You already bitching about the job, Jayden? Is all this work cutting into your dating time?" Damon stepped out from the locker room wearing low-hanging gym shorts and a whole lot of sweat. He had one boxing glove tucked under his arm while he untied the other with his free hand and teeth.

Jayden crossed his arms and leaned against the wall. "Just trying to keep the ladies happy." Jayden smirked as he told the lie without flinching. It was a talent he had recently learned to master.

Damon snorted. "You keep showing up for work looking like a female has kept you up all night and Barrett just might ship your ass back to Louisiana."

Jayden straightened, his smile slipping a little before he remembered to adjust it. "Has Barrett been complaining about my job performance?" He needed this job more than anything.

Damon pulled his other glove off and shook his head. "Hell, no. He's pretty impressed that you're taking the job as a Guardian so seriously." Damon narrowed his eyes. "Plus the fact that you're the first one to volunteer for overtime has him drooling at the mouth. But if I were you I'd go easy on the brown-nosing, brother."

Jayden laughed. "It's called taking up the slack, not brown-nosing. You'd do well to learn the art, my friend, and pick up some overtime yourself."

Damon grinned and shook his head, sending droplets of sweat raining down onto the floor. "No, thanks. I've got Ava waiting on me at five o'clock sharp at the door with nothing on." Damon reached down and adjusted himself and Jayden could tell the Were was getting aroused just talking about his woman.

An unexpected jolt of jealously hit Jayden in the gut. He'd

never expected Damon to be mated at all, let alone be mated before him.

"Being mated looks good on you, Damon."

Damon straightened and held out his hand. "Thanks, brother."

Jayden shook his hand and pulled away. "I got a meeting with Barrett and I don't want to be late." As he walked away, Damon called after him.

"Just wait, Jayden. Once you're mated you'll be trying to find someone else to pick up your overtime too."

JAYDEN WALKED up to Barrett's steel door and knocked. Barrett's office, like the rest of the compound, was built like a fucking tank. Reinforced steel and concrete. After a bomb that took out a building some months back, they'd made sure to make the building was as bomb proof as possible.

"Come in, Jayden," Barrett's booming voice called out from the other side of the door.

A shiver ran up his back as he opened the heavy door and walked in. It was freaky how Barrett had this sixth sense of knowing who was on the other side of the door without even looking. Jayden often wondered if the Pack Master could see inside Jayden's head as well.

He lifted his chin in greeting as Barrett motioned for him to sit in the chair across from his desk. Barrett continued studying a pile of papers in a brown folder.

Jayden eased into the leather chair that looked so out of place in the dreary room. The cinderblock walls looked more like a jail cell than an office. Even Barrett's worn and scarred desk looked like he had bought it from the yard sale of a retired attorney. The walls held no pictures, except for one elaborate shield with the Arkansas state flag and the words, "LEADER

AND COMMANDER BORN TO UPHOLD THE LUPINE
LAW."

Jayden fidgeted in his seat, the mood in the room growing heavier with each passing second. The other jobs that Barrett had assigned him had taken no more than a minute of discussion to find out the details before he was out the door.

Whatever papers Barrett was currently focused on had an uneasiness crawling up his spine.

"I see that your interior decorator has been on vacay," Jayden joked as he looked around the room.

Barrett cut his eyes at him.

Jayden sat up straighter. Not that he was a pussy, but Jayden always got this lethal vibe off Barrett, like at any minute he could rip your throat out and then sit politely down and have a mocha latte.

"My decorator is dead."

Shit. "I'm sorry." Jayden swallowed and made sure there wasn't a smirk lingering on his lips.

"Don't be. I killed him." Barrett lifted his head, fixing his blue-eyed stare on Jayden.

"Well, if he made my office look like shit, I'd kill him too." Jayden cringed. He always did have a hard time holding his tongue.

Barrett cracked the slightest of smiles. A rare sight indeed.

"I have a new assignment that is going to need your utmost attention."

Jayden leaned forward. Now they were talking. "Absolutely. Whatcha got?"

Barrett sat back in his chair and steepled his fingers. "It's Haley Guthrie."

Jayden felt the blood drain from his face. "What about her?"

"It seems that she has picked up a stalker." Barrett pushed the folder towards him. "It started a week after she moved into the dorm."

Jayden picked up the first note. It read *"Hello beautiful. Hope you have a wonderful day."* He met Barrett's gaze and shrugged. "Could be just an infatuated guy. And if gets more serious, just order her back to LSU."

Barrett narrowed his eyes. "It's more than an infatuated guy with a crush. And her parents are the reason she's not at LSU anymore."

Jayden looked up. "What do you mean?"

"When we rescued Haley, her parents weren't exactly excited to have their precious little girl home." Barrett narrowed his eyes as he eased back into his chair, never once taking his focus off Jayden.

"Why the hell not?" Anger flared in Jayden's gut at Barrett's words.

"It seems, in their eyes, Haley has brought shame to their family. To them, a raped female werewolf is ruined. Damaged goods." Barrett's voice vibrated with utter distaste for Haley's parents. Jayden's hatred for them doubled.

"How could a parent do that?" Jayden snarled.

"To some in this world, appearances mean everything." Barrett stood and walked over to the far wall and flipped a switch. The wall slid away on a track revealing a secret interior room.

Jayden followed Barrett inside. This room was vastly different from the Pack Master's office. TV screens lined the wall, each capturing a different surveillance camera within the city. There were at least five computers along with monitors lined up on the stainless steel desks. There were no windows and only one way in and out. It appeared to be a safe room of some sort.

Barrett walked over to the far side of the room where a

large map of the state of Arkansas hung on the wall, littered with colored stickpins. He pointed to the bright red pig that had been stuck on the city of Fayetteville.

Jayden chuckled.

LSU had their tigers. University of Arkansas had their razorbacks.

"So if she is being stalked then why not just move her to another state?" Jayden curled his hands into fists.

"I believe he's dangerous and will follow her wherever she goes." Jayden crossed his arms over his chest. The hair on the back of his neck was standing up and he knew whatever was about to come out of Barrett's mouth wasn't good.

"Stalkers like this usually turn out to be serial killers." Barrett turned back to him.

Jayden's heart sped up. His fingernails cut into his palms, he knew if he looked he would see blood trickling out from the wound. The urge to shift into wolf swamped him in a rush.

CHAPTER 2

"How long has this been going on? Has Haley gone to the police?" Jayden forced himself to keep his voice calm despite the volatile storm raging inside.

"It started when she arrived at the University of Arkansas. She went to the campus police, but they said they couldn't do anything, since they don't know who it is. I sent a couple of Guardians down to Louisiana to investigate the ex-boyfriend."

"Ex?" Jayden knew she had a boyfriend. The night she was kidnapped she was on her way to visit him. She'd left LSU to go visit him at his home in Lafayette.

Barrett seared him with a glare. "Apparently Mommy and Daddy aren't the only assholes concerned about damaged goods. That little prick dumped her the second he found out what happened."

Anger surged through his entire system making him wish he had a bad guy, drug dealer, kidnapper—any would do—in front of him so he could rip them apart with his teeth.

"My money is on the boyfriend. He might be regretting

what he lost and is now making her pay for it." Jayden looked away before Barrett could see the yellow-orange tint to his pupils, signaling the shift into wolf. He needed to get it together. He didn't need to be out of control in front of his new Pack Master.

The last thing he needed was to shift in front of Barrett. Being a Guardian meant being in control of yourself at all times. Humans, except for the government, didn't know werewolves existed outside of novels and movies. Hell, humans had enough to keep them fearful: global warming, sucky economy, and episodes of reality TV.

"Okay, so what do you need from me? Gathering Intel? Asking around at the college? Surveillance?" Every muscle in his body trembled with the urge to find whoever was scaring Haley and make them pay in blood. He could most certainly make it look like an accident, or at least an animal attack.

"All of the above. I have a house in Fayetteville. I stay there when the Razorbacks are playing. You'll stay there. I've talked to Haley and told her I will have someone in place protecting her while she goes to her classes."

"Have you told her she will have to stop going to parties with her friends at night?"

Barrett arched a brow. "What parties? She gave me her daily schedule and the only time she leaves her room is to go to class. Her roommate, Dana, is the only friend she's made since moving to Fayetteville. Hell, she doesn't even go out to eat. She eats every meal in her room."

Jayden scowled. Was she as fucked up as him over what had happened? Had he done this to her by not being able to save her?

"You okay with this assignment?" Barrett gave him a long assessing look.

"Yeah." Jayden gave a quick nod.

"Good. I'm counting on you to keep that girl safe. God

knows we're the only family she's got now." Jayden swallowed.

He had failed Haley once.

Whatever it took, he wasn't going to fail her again.

"Holy shit, here comes Barrett Middleton." Dana spoke out of the side of her mouth, as they stood on the sidewalk outside the boutique in the town square. "I wonder if he caught me trying to sneak a peek at him in the Guardian's gym?"

Haley almost stopped breathing when she spotted Barrett Middleton headed straight for her. She had come to him under the cover of night to explain her situation and show him the letters. As her new Pack Master, Barrett was her last resort for protection.

She had screwed up every last ounce of courage to actually walk into the Guardian building. When a large werewolf with a scar across his cheek had stepped in front of her, she was sure her heart had stopped. For a brief second she had wondered if her parents would even come to her funeral.

His name was Damon and he'd pierced her with a glare before leading her to Barrett's office.

While Dana knew about the first few notes she'd gotten, she didn't know about the latest one, the ones that had her lying awake all night wondering if she was going to live another day. Even though Dana was a werewolf, Haley hadn't told her what had happened in Louisiana or the real reason behind why she transferred colleges. She didn't want her friend to disappear like her family had.

"Hello, ladies." Barrett nodded and turned his gaze on her friend. "Dana, how is college going? Not partying too much are you?"

Dana blushed. "It's going good. Keeping my grades up and staying out of trouble."

"Good, good." Barrett turned back to Haley. "Are you going to introduce me to your friend?"

"Oh, shoot, of course." Dana laughed. "This is Haley

Guthrie. She just transferred to the university from LSU."

Barrett stuck out his hand and Haley blinked. Of course Dana wouldn't have a clue that she'd already met the Pack Master.

Haley accepted his outstretched hand.

"Nice to meet you, Haley. I think you will find the Weres in Arkansas welcoming and very protective of their own," Barrett said.

Haley's heart hitched at his underlying meaning. She'd lived in Louisiana all her life, but her own family had failed to protect her or even accept her after she had been hurt. Even the Pack Master of Louisiana had refused to see her when she went to him about what had happened the night of her kidnapping.

Yet standing here on the sidewalk in front of the whole town, Barrett Middleton, the Pack Master himself, had sought her out. And promised his protection.

Haley blinked back the tears burning the back of her eyes and cleared her throat. "Thank you, Mr. Middleton. I appreciate that."

"I see you two are heading back to Fayetteville." Barrett turned to Dana. "Dana, do you mind running across the street to Hilda Mae's bakery? I believe she has a welcome basket for

Haley with lots of her homemade cookies."

"I'll be happy to." Dana gave Barrett a besotted smile. "I'll be right back."

Barrett folded his arms and looked across the town square as he spoke in a hushed tone. To anyone passing by it would appear they were talking about something as innocent as the weather.

"I have one of my men following you back to Fayetteville. Dana won't notice. She's too busy trying to get a glance at me while I'm working out." Haley's face heated.

"My Guardian will be following you to class and back to the dorm to make sure you are safe. If you get another letter, text me and I'll have him pick it up."

"I don't have your number." Haley dug around in her purse to find her cell phone.

"I already put it in your phone." Barrett glanced at her and the looked away.

"When?" Haley tried to keep from showing her surprise.

"The other night. When you were in my office."

She remembered dumping out her purse contents which held the letters. She'd been desperate to the point of tears when she was asking him for help. He must have slipped his number into her phone then.

"Thank you." It came out as a slip of a whisper as emotion clogged her throat.

"Don't thank me. It's what we do. I don't want you to feel like you're alone anymore, Haley. Because you're not. We protect our own."

Dana stepped out of the bakery, her arms loaded with a large basket filled to the brim with baked pastries and cookies. The basket was so large that Dana had to hold it up to check for traffic before crossing the street.

"Don't say anything to Dana about this. The less she knows the better. If you have problems or feel unsafe, text me and I'll have my Guardian come get you. He will only be a few feet away during the day and five minutes away at night."

"Thank you." Haley swallowed, as a weight lifted off her

shoulders. "You don't know how much I appreciate this. If there is anything I can ever do to repay you. Let me know."

"Actually there is. Don't let Dana know you have my number. And tell her to stay out of the Guardian's house." Barrett shot Dana a wave before he walked away.

"I didn't get to say goodbye." Dana huffed as she reached Haley.

Haley looked at her friend.

"He is totally hot." Dana licked her lips a little.

"You don't find him scary?" Haley looked at Barrett's large retreating back. Sure the man was built like a model, but there was something so intense that it intimidated her.

"Of course I find him scary. Scary and hot. I wouldn't mind if he tied me to his bed and spanked me." Dana purred.

"Tell me how you really feel." Haley snorted.

Dana looked at Haley and laughed. "I can't help it. I need some alone time with my honey. My fantasies are all I have."

Haley opened the door to the backseat of her car and stuck the basket on the seat. "Not anymore. You ordered all that sex stuff from Granny." She adjusted the seatbelt around the basket.

"Maybe I'll break it in with a good fantasy starring Barrett."

"Enough." Haley stuck her fingers in her ears and hummed, trying to ignore the visual.

Dana straightened and frowned. "What were you two talking about anyway? I don't think I've ever seen Barrett make a point of talking to someone on the sidewalk. He's rarely comes out of his office."

Haley pressed her lips into a thin line.

"I know that look. Spill it. What did Barrett say?" Dana crossed her arms.

Haley blew out a breath. She wasn't going to say

anything, she really wasn't. But she didn't really have a choice.

"Barrett said for you to stop trying to peep into the Guardian's gym while he's working out."

CHAPTER 3

*F*or three days Jayden arrived on the campus of University of Arkansas early enough to find a position out of sight, yet near enough he could intervene if Haley was in danger.

For three days he followed her as she went from her dorm to her classes.

For three days Jayden had observed her manner and demeanor as she so desperately attempted to blend in to the crowd and not draw attention to herself.

And for three days nothing happened.

Jayden lifted the Styrofoam cup to his lips. The steam rolled out of the top and he blew it a little before taking a sip of the bitter, gas station coffee. The door to the dorm opened and his gaze locked on Haley as she walked to her first class of the day. The spring breeze caught her blonde hair and lifted it into the air. Her delicate hand brushed a strand of yellow silk out of her eyes.

Jayden frowned. Even from this distance he could see the faint dark circles under her eyes.

She wasn't sleeping.

This would explain the drop in her grades.

Jayden hadn't left the campus until late last night, watching for anything out of the ordinary. He saw nothing. So he spent the rest of the night on the computer hacking into the university's database, gathering any information he could find on Haley. Her grades had progressively spiraled downward and even her teachers had commented on her withdrawal from participating in class. Where she had once been a dedicated student, she was now showing signs of disinterest, possibly failing out of college completely.

That pissed him off. The stalker was now controlling her life as well as affecting her future.

Jayden eased closer as Haley headed for the entrance of the building where her last class was held. She hurried past a group of college guys, head down, her fingers clutching her backpack like a lifeline.

"Hey, beautiful." One guy wearing a bright orange T-shirt called out to her.

Haley kept her head down as she walked. Jayden's gut clenched as he tossed the Styrofoam cup into the nearest garbage can and hurried near.

He had been given strict orders to stay back and watch, only revealing himself to Haley in an emergency. But when he saw her blue-eyed gaze dart nervously, and how she clutched the straps of her backpack in a white-fingered grip, the only thing he could think of was protecting her from the group of assholes.

"What's your hurry?" The guy reached out and grabbed her arm. Haley stared up at him, eyes wide with fear.

"Fuck the orders." Jayden murmured as he stalked right up and pulled the guy's hand off Haley.

"Get your fucking hands off my girl." Jayden stepped in front of Haley, hands fisted ready to fight.

The guy's eyes widened as he took in Jayden's large size.

Werewolves were bigger and more muscular than normal humans. As much as he liked intimidating humans, he much preferred the feel of bone cracking under his fists.

"Sorry, man. I didn't know she was dating anyone." The guy held up his hands as he backed away with the rest of his friends.

Keep it moving, motherfuckers. Jayden growled behind clenched teeth, restraining the wolf within.

Jayden watched the group of guys head to the safety of their cars before turning to face Haley.

She was nowhere in sight.

CHAPTER 4

"Fuck." He hurried up the steps into the building she'd just left and peeked into every classroom. He couldn't find her anywhere.

According to his notes, the only other place she ever went was her dorm room. When he researched Haley and which dorm she stayed in he had been surprised to discover it was coed. Since she'd transferred in mid-semester, she didn't get a choice of dorms. He jogged over to her building, ignoring the appreciative stares and smiles from the silly college girls he'd passed.

He entered the dormitory hall, and a sense of déjà vu washed over him. He had blown it in college. What did he expect when he partied all the time, skipped classes and chased too many girls? He'd been young and dumb, been more concerned with getting into girls' panties than getting a college education. He still remembered the day he was called into the dean's office and kicked out. The worst part was going home to face Granny. The look of disappointment on her face about killed him.

Not getting a college degree was one of his regrets in life.

If he could go back and do things differently he would have studied harder, maybe gone into computer programming. He was good at the tech stuff.

Ignoring the flirty looks from the girls he passed in the hall, he continued on until he found Haley's room. He took a deep breath and knocked. He had probably scared her half to death when he got all aggressive with those guys. He couldn't blame her.

She cracked the door. She stared back at him, locks of blonde hair shielding half her face. He nodded, impressed that she didn't just throw open the door without knowing who was on the other side.

"Jayden, what are you doing here?" She looked only slightly less scared than when the college guy grabbed her.

Fucking perfect.

"Haley, we need to talk." Jayden lowered his voice and looked both ways down the hall. With the exception of two girls heading for their rooms, it was virtually empty.

He glanced back at her, wondering how long she was going to keep him standing out in the hall like an idiot.

"Barrett sent me." He leaned in and lowered his voice. "I'm here to help."

Her eyes widened for a fraction of a second and then she closed the door. The chain rattled before the door swung open. She stepped back, allowing him entrance.

He hesitated. "We could go to the coffee shop and talk. We don't have to do this here." Being in her room was way too intimate. He didn't want to make her any more uncomfortable than she already was.

Haley shook her head fervently. "No. I'd rather talk here. Come on in."

He stepped inside, filling the tiny room with his large frame. There were two twin beds, each with its own nightstand and desk, all university standard furniture. One side of the room was decorated with posters of rock bands and half naked men and the bed decorated with a bright pink and black comforter. The other half, Haley's side, was neatly decorated, with a couple of abstract paintings on the wall and a solid taupe comforter with a dozen brightly colored pillows all in various shades of blue and green.

They might be roommates, but they had totally different personalities.

Haley sat down on her bed watching Jayden glance around the room as he shoved his hands in his jean pockets. She smoothed her coverlet with her fingers, hoping he wouldn't see the slight tremble. The incident outside had shaken her more than she wanted him to know.

"My roommate, Dana, shouldn't be back for a while. She still has class for the next few hours. I'm assuming, since you just blew your cover, you suspect that guy you just confronted is the one that has been sending me all those letters." Haley wrapped her arms around her chest.

"No, I blew my cover because he had his hands on you." Jayden glanced away and ran his fingers through his blonde hair. It was longer than what she remembered in Louisiana, a couple inches past his shoulders. But his eyes, boy oh boy, his blue eyes were exactly the same, like the Mediterranean Sea.

And right now those blue eyes were aimed right at her.

"You want to tell me what's going on?" He narrowed his gaze.

"You know as much as I do, assuming Barrett told filled you in on everything." She shrugged and glanced away. He was acting like this was her fault, her doing. Like she was asking for it.

Jayden shook his head and his frown deepened. "I'm

talking about how you manage to let someone else control your life."

Haley's mouth dropped open. "What are you talking about?"

"I'm talking about the only time you leave this room is to go to class. You don't hang out with your friends, or go to bars, or even go to any games. Hell, you don't even eat in the cafeteria." Haley shook her head, a spark of anger starting to burn deep within her chest. "I can't do any of those things. How do I know he won't be there, watching me, waiting for me?" Did he not understand anything?

"I understand that you're scared…"

"Do you, Jayden? Do you know what it's like to be disowned by your family, to have no one you can talk to? Not even your roommate? Because if you tell your roommate then you might be putting her in danger too? Do you know what it's like to have your life turned upside down? To not be able to sleep at night, constantly worried that if he is close enough to put note on my door, then he is close enough to get into my room?" Her voice started to build with each pointed question fired at him. She stood and stepped into his personal space.

"Do you know what it's like to finally tell someone, which happened to be Barrett, who isn't exactly Mr. Warm and Fuzzy, about some psycho who won't stop messing with your mind?" Haley gasped and slapped her hand over her mouth. She'd said way too much. Her knees buckled as she sunk down on her bed.

"You are absolutely right. I don't know." Jayden eased down on Dana's bed across from her. He probably thought she was bat shit crazy.

She didn't blame him. Lately she'd felt crazy.

"I didn't mean to scare you." Jayden scowled as he gazed down on the floor.

"You didn't scare me." She'd never been frightened of Jayden.

He looked up at her. "Why did you go back to your dorm? Why didn't you just go on to your other classes?"

Haley shrugged. "I don't know. I guess I was shocked to see you. When Barrett said he was sending someone to watch me I thought it would be someone I didn't know."

"So you didn't think I was the stalker?" Jayden cut his gaze at her.

Haley snorted. "Ah, no. It was perfectly clear when I saw you at your grandmother's house you couldn't get away from me fast enough. Stalkers tend to want to be near their victims."

Jayden stared at her for so long that she had to look away. She stood and walked over to her desk and snatched up her phone. "Look, nothing has happened since I got back. Maybe I was making a big deal out of nothing. I can call Barrett and tell him that I don't need anyone."

He stood and grabbed her phone out of her hand. "Don't call him. It's only been a few days." He set her phone down on the desk. "What time do you usually get the notes?"

"I usually find them on my door when I get back from class." She crossed her arms over her chest. "Why?"

"So you've never had one delivered when you were here in the room?"

She shook her head. "No, never. Why are you looking at me like that? What's wrong?"

Jayden tensed, his senses going wild. The back of his neck crawled and he couldn't shake the feeling that they were being watched. He tried the window making sure it was locked. He looked out. The shrubbery was so dense it would make it impossible for someone to even get near the window.

"What's wrong? What is it?" Haley came up beside him, her gaze darting nervously out the window and then back at him.

He could smell her fear filling the tiny room.

He pressed his finger to her lips, alerting her to be quiet. She silently nodded. He eased to the door and carefully unhooked the chain. Gripping the knob, he flung open the door.

A white envelope that had been wedged into the door, fluttered to the floor. He glanced down the hall. The hallway was empty except for a lone guy wearing a bathrobe and flip flops on making his way down the hall.

"Stay in this room!" Jayden called out over his shoulder before he ran down the hallway. He tackled the half-naked guy to the linoleum floor. The guy landed with a thunk.

"Hey man! What the fuck!"

"Did you put that note on Haley Guthrie's door?" Jayden pulled the guy up from the floor and slammed him against the wall. Pinning him to the wall with his hand to his sternum, Jayden glared at the guy, watching for any hint of a lie.

"I don't know who you're talking about, dude." The guy's eyes widened in fear as he struggled to get away.

"Did you see anyone else in the hall?" He leaned in and lowered his voice.

"No! I just got out of the shower, man. I swear!" The guy flailed in the air, trying to get his feet to touch the ground.

Jayden knew from the male's scent that the guy was telling the truth. Whoever had left that envelope must have hauled ass before anyone could see him.

Jayden took a step back and let the guy slide down the wall. He landed on his feet but his robe gaped open. He must have scared the guy pretty good because he definitely had some major shrinkage going on.

Jayden shook his head and walked back to Haley's door. Scooping up the letter with the corner of his T-shirt, he knocked on the door. "Haley open up. It's me."

The door swung open and he was met with her wide-eyed gaze. Jayden ushered her back inside the safety of the room.

"Do you have a plastic bag?"

She nodded and went over to a trunk at the foot of her bed. She rummaged through the contents before handing him a clear plastic sandwich bag.

Jayden retrieved the knife from his boot and slit the top of the envelope. He knew he should have left the damn thing alone until Barrett could check it for prints. But he needed to know what it said. He had to.

Haley stepped closer, trying to look around him. Her firm breasts pressed into his back, and sent his blood humming. He closed his eyes and struggled to breathe.

"I need to look at it first okay?" Jayden hoped she would back up. Anger and arousal bombarded him like he was in a fucking war zone. He was mad as hell that he hadn't heard the stalker leave the note. He was frustrated that he had managed to blow his cover. And he was confused and so fucking hard at being near Haley it made him sick to his stomach.

When she stepped away, he drew an easy breath.

Touching only the edges of the folded notebook paper, he opened it

'You shouldn't have let that man into your room. You should have told him that you belong to me. In life and death, Haley.'

A growl slipped past his lips as possessive lust filled every cell of his body.

"What is it? What does it say?" Haley grabbed his arm and made him face her.

"Get your stuff. You're not staying here."

Haley sat in the front seat of Jayden's black Mustang, watching as he stuffed all her meager belongings into the trunk of the car. Whatever was in that letter had put Jayden on edge.

"It must be something bad. Something really, really bad."

She had let her dorm ambassador know she was moving out and left a note for Dana as well.

She shot Jayden a look as he slid into the driver's seat with a sexy ease. His blond hair brushed his shoulders as he reached to turn the key in the ignition. He looked sexy without even trying.

"So I guess I'm dropping out of college?" Perfect. Her life was now officially over. She had no family and now no way to support herself.

"Nope. You're still going to classes. You're just not going to live in the dorm anymore."

"Dana's going to be mad that I didn't explain in person." Haley looked out her window and bit her lip. Dana was her first and only friend that she made when she transferred to Arkansas. She was lucky that Dana happened to be wolf like her.

"No, she won't. I added that you left because we have been secretly dating and decided to move in together, since I moved to Fayetteville." He pulled his car onto the street. The muscle car roared down the street as he increased the speed.

Haley jerked her head towards him. "You did what?"

"Stop looking at me like that. Girls date older guys all the time. How old are you anyway?"

When she didn't say anything, he shook his head. "Okay fine, I'll go first. I'm thirty."

"Really? I didn't think you were that old." He looked like a college student himself.

"Stop avoiding the question. How old are you, Haley?" He shot her a glare.

"Twenty-four. I would have already graduated from college if I didn't change my major two years ago." Jayden nodded thoughtfully.

"My parents got married when my mom was only sixteen and my dad was thirty." Werewolves looked at age differently than humans. Once you found your mate, you were with them forever, regardless of age.

Jayden gawked. "You're kidding, right?"

"Nope." She patted him on the back and gave him a forced smile. "That should make you feel better. At least I'm a legal consenting adult."

He continued to stare at her like she'd grown two heads. His car veered off the street and his tire grazed the side of the road. She screamed.

"Sorry, sorry. " He righted the car and kept his attention straight ahead.

He made a turn on to a quaint street and slowed down. When he pulled into the driveway of a cottage-style home, she cut her gaze at him.

"What's wrong? You don't like it?" Jayden looked from the house back to her.

"You really did move to Fayetteville." Why would he have done that? Why wouldn't he have just rented a hotel room?

A slight smile tugged at his lips. "Nah. It's Barrett's house. He stays here when the Razorbacks are playing in town. That dude is a serious football addict." He cut the engine and got out.

"Well, it's the South. It's kind of expected," she muttered.

Jayden opened her car door just as she reached for the handle. She blushed as she walked around to the trunk of the car. It had been a long time since a guy opened a door for her.

It took them one trip to bring her stuff into the house. After piling it all into one of the bedrooms, she took the opportunity to look around.

The house was small, probably no more than twelve hundred square feet. It was an older home, but it looked like everything had been remodeled and updated. New windows had been put in, the walls had been painted modern colors, and the heart of pine floors had been refinished. She wandered into the kitchen. It too had been remodeled. The cabinets were new and white, the countertops dark granite, and the appliances had been updated to stainless steel.

"This is totally not what I expected Barrett's house to be." Haley cut her eyes at Jayden.

"I know, right. Doesn't look very manly." Jayden snorted.

"Maybe he had someone decorate it." She couldn't imagine the lethal Pack Master picking out wall paint colors and throw pillows.

"Ah, that would be a definite no. I heard his decorator... passed away."

"Oh, well maybe his girlfriend did it." Haley cocked her head and faced Jayden. "Does Barrett have a girlfriend?"

Jayden wrinkled his nose. "Ah, that would be a definite no. I don't think I've ever seen him out with a woman."

"Well, maybe he's gay."

"Absolutely not!"

Haley crossed her arms. "How can you be so sure?"

Jayden stared at her for a second. "Because his screen

saver has a half-naked model on it." Jayden leaned closer and smiled. "She wasn't wearing any clothes, just a pair of wings."

Haley's breath caught in her throat at his nearness. Jayden's scent of ocean and wind seemed to curl around her like smoke. She couldn't help herself as she leaned slightly in to him.

She'd always been attracted to him, even on that first night when he'd come to rescue her, but when he didn't try to find her afterwards, she'd quickly gotten the message that he wasn't interested.

She sucked in a breath as she met his intense gaze. If he didn't want to be near her, why was he looking at her like he wanted to eat her alive?

A smirk froze on his full lips, his pupils dilated. He cocked his head to the side, letting his gaze drift down to her lips. Her heart thumped against her chest as she saw something dangerously close to lust emerge behind his blue eyes.

She held her breath waiting for him to kiss her.

He straightened and cleared his throat, as his expression hardened. "I need to go see what's in the kitchen for dinner."

Without so much as a glance, he walked away, leaving her alone with her conflicted feelings.

"What the fuck is wrong with me?" Jayden snarled out as he white-knuckled the kitchen sink and looked out the window into fenced backyard. He had almost made the biggest mistake of his career as a Guardian by giving into his instincts and kissing Haley Guthrie. He knew it wouldn't have stopped there. He wanted more than just a kiss.

He shook his head, shocked and repulsed at his loss of self-control. Shit, if Barrett found out, he'd kick his ass out of Arkansas faster than hell. Then where would he be?

He sucked in a deep breath to clear his head and glanced down at the tent in his crotch. He was so fucking hard, any second his dick was going to rip through his zipper. She stirred up his body unlike any other female he'd ever been around. The problem was her age. She was twenty-four, for fuck's sake. He never dated anyone that young before. He preferred his females knowledgeable when it came to sex. He didn't have the patience to teach her how to pleasure him. Yet he couldn't deny how quickly he'd gotten aroused from just being near her.

He tightened his hold on the edge of the counter as blood pounded in his veins. Hell, he'd guess the only experience Haley had with sex was that dickhead boyfriend and then what that rogue wolf had done to her when she'd been kidnapped. She needed someone gentle, someone sweet.

He rubbed the back of his neck, remembering the feel of vertebra cracking under his hand as he snapped the neck of the first wolf that tried to rape her. After that, Jayden had been captured and dragged out before he could kill the second wolf in the room.

What he needed was to get laid. It had been months since he'd last had sex. Hell, it had been that long since he'd even had an erection. Until now.

"I'm going to take a bath," Haley called out as she made her way toward the bathroom.

"Take your time." Jayden closed his eyes as he heard a door shut and the water turn on. He imagined her sliding out of that sweatshirt and jeans. What color underwear and bra would she be wearing? Angel white? Or devil red?

He opened his eyes as he stroked his erection through his jeans. His body came alive so fast it shocked him. He could almost hear her stepping into the water and sinking down into the warm bath.

He reached for his zipper. He was a sick bastard. But damn, he needed some kind of relief before he went crazy. He'd never been this this hard in his entire life.

Closing his hand around his cock, he slowly stroked, visualizing the naked image of Haley spreading her thighs for him like a present.

He could imagine how she'd gasp when he tried to enter her tight heat. She'd tighten around him with delicious pleasure until he was all the way inside.

He stroked himself harder and faster until he let out a groan, spilling his release onto the kitchen floor.

Jayden shuddered, disgusted at himself. Something was wrong with him. He shouldn't be fantasizing about someone he couldn't have.

He snatched up some paper towels and quickly cleaned up his mess. Shoving the paper towels and the evidence in the garbage can, he washed his hands. With his body under control, he made a mental note to call Barrett and update him on the situation.

If his Pack Master knew what was best, then maybe he'd send someone to replace him. Before things got out of hand and boundaries were crossed.

"Haley."

"Go away." She swatted the hand on her shoulder that was shaking her and interrupting her sleep.

"Haley, wake up." Jayden's voice drifted over her.

"What time is it?" She blinked and forced open her leaden eyes. Jayden sat on the edge of the bed, looming over her with his large presence.

"Seven." Jayden stared down at her.

"Seven a.m.?" She bolted upright. She couldn't afford to miss class. Her unblemished attendance was the only thing keeping her from failing out of college.

"No. It's seven o'clock at night. Dinner's ready." He chuckled.

Haley pushed herself up on her elbows and hid a yawn behind her hand. "That bath must have made me sleepy." She hadn't slept that well since she'd moved to Arkansas. She eased off the bed and stood.

"Have you been sleeping at night?" Jayden asked as they walked down the hall toward the kitchen.

"Not really." She shrugged. The fact was she hadn't slept more than a few hours at a time. She was surprised that she could still function. It was probably all the adrenaline pumping through her body from being constantly on guard.

He motioned for her to sit at the small kitchen island and placed a plate in front of her. Her mouth watered as the delicious aroma assaulted her senses.

"I'm guessing you like steak." Jayden shot her a grin. Her heart raced a little in her chest. *Get over yourself, girl. He's just here to do his job, not do you.*

"I'm Were, aren't I?" She eyed the plate with appreciation. "Did you make all this?"

"It doesn't take much skill to make a salad and bake a potato. Grilling a steak is something all guys know how to do."

Haley snorted. "You should tell that to my ex-boyfriend."

His eyes narrowed at the mention of her ex. He turned and opened the refrigerator.

"All I got is beer." He held up a long neck bottle that he pulled from the fridge.

"Beer works for me." She smirked as his eyebrow shot up.

"Jayden, I have been drinking since long before I was legal. My parents practically raised me on wine." That wasn't entirely true, but there wasn't a night at the Guthrie house that wine wasn't served. When she turned fifteen her parents had let her have a glass with her dinner.

She could sense that even though she was well over legal age, Jayden thought she wasn't as mature as the girls he normally dated.

He finally handed her a beer. She took a drink, letting the icy beverage slide down her parched throat.

She might not be his type, but she certainly was far more mature than he was giving her credit for. And the only way for him to realize that was to see for himself.

Jayden sat across the kitchen island from Haley. He couldn't stop himself from watching as she ate her first bite of meat.

"*Mmmm*. That's really good." She sighed. "I haven't had steak in months."

"I hear there are some good steak restaurants here in

Fayetteville."

"Really? I guess I haven't had the opportunity to find out."

Jayden frowned. College was supposed to be an experience of a lifetime and some asshole was taking those moments away from her, keeping her living in fear and isolation.

"How long have you been getting the notes?" Jayden took a long drink and studied her.

She brushed her blonde hair out of her eyes and set her fork down. "The first note came a few weeks after I transferred here." She shrugged. "I didn't think anything about it because it was so generic and innocent. I actually thought it was Dana's boyfriend, Mark, leaving her notes. When I asked Dana about them she said that Mark hadn't written them."

"Mark Boulland is enrolled in the medical program, right?"

"Yeah. How'd you know that?" Haley gave him a surprised look.

"I had to research everyone who might be a potential suspect. Usually stalkers have a personal relationship with their victims." He tried to keep his tone casual, so as not to scare her. She needed to know that he would do whatever it took to keep her safe. He wouldn't fail her again.

Haley shook her head. "I don't think it's anyone I know. At least not any of my friends."

Jayden shrugged. "You could be right." But he wasn't taking any chances. While she had been asleep, he'd called Barrett and told him he had moved Haley into the house to keep her safe. His commander wasn't exactly pleased, but Jayden didn't apologize for it. He had also updated his Pack Master about the note she'd gotten and shipped it to Barrett so he could check it for prints.

Haley gazed longingly out the kitchen window.

She looked so sad, like she was caught between her fear of what might happen and wanting to live her life.

"You want to go sit out back? It's pretty private and the fence is secure. No one can see you or get in."

"I'd love to." Her eyes sparkled like he'd just given her a present. She'd lost the simple joy of enjoying a spring night.

It fueled his rage at the asshole that was stalking Haley. She didn't deserve this.

When Jayden caught him, and he would catch him, he was going to make sure he paid with his life.

After dinner, they stepped out onto the wooden deck with their beers and were greeted with the heavy scent of jasmine and azaleas hanging in the air. They sat in the Adirondack lounge chairs, both silently appreciating the peacefulness. The sun dipped below the horizon leaving only the faint purple light of twilight in its wake. The gentle evening breeze caressed her blonde hair and Jayden caught her scent on the wind. He wanted to dig his fingers through the silky strands and bury his face in her neck and breathe her in.

"I've missed this. Being able to sit outside, especially now that it's warm." She stared up into the sky, a soft smile on her lips.

"There's an outdoor concert Saturday at the park. It's supposed to be perfect weather. We could take a cooler of beer and a blanket." Jayden watched Haley's face light up for the briefest of seconds before her expression sobered.

"I don't think that's a good idea." She looked away and wrapped her arms around herself.

"I think it's a perfect idea. I'll be there. You'll be safe." He knew she needed this, needed to get out of the house and start living again.

Her brow creased as she contemplated his promise of safety. He could tell she was thinking too much about her safety.

"I'll be right back." Jayden stood and walked in the house. He came out with his phone and portable speaker. "How about some music?"

"Sure." She smiled.

He connected the speaker to the phone and turned on his playlist. Easing into the chair, he pillowed his hands behind his head to stare up at the sky.

"Did you go to college?" She turned and looked at him.

"Yep. LSU." He cut a glance at her. "I majored in partying and minored in getting laid."

She laughed and for the first time, Jayden saw real joy in her eyes. No fear, no worry, just joy.

"No, really. I flunked out." He took a drink of his beer. "Do you miss LSU?"

"I don't know." She shrugged. "Both my parents went there so it was always expected of me to go there as well. Didn't really have a choice."

"Is that where you met your boyfriend, at LSU?" Jayden swallowed. The word boyfriend left a bitter taste in his mouth.

"Anthony? Yep. He was older so we were only at college together for a year." She took a sip and stared up at the sky.

"Do you miss him?" Why the hell did he ask that? "Never mind. I didn't mean to get too personal." He scrubbed his hand across his face. Thank God it was dark so she couldn't see him blushing like a pussy.

"It's okay. When I first moved I missed him. But not now." Her expression hardened.

"Haley do you think, he could be having someone leave the notes? Maybe he is upset because you transferred?"

Haley snorted and took a long drink. "He's the one that broke up with me. I assure you Anthony isn't the stalker."

Jayden shook his head. He knew that Barrett was keeping tabs on the ex to see if Anthony had attempted to contact someone in Fayetteville to do his dirty work. It wouldn't be that hard to stalk someone long distance. Jayden also knew the ex was filthy rich and could afford to pay a lackey to keep his mouth shut and continue harassing Haley.

"Usually females are stalked by their ex-boyfriend. If he regrets letting you go and you refused to get back together, then that sets up the perfect scenario for stalking. It's almost textbook." No one would be stupid enough to let her go.

Haley stood and glared at Jayden.

"It's not him."

"Haley, I'm looking at this from all angles." Jayden stood and held up his hands. Women had a tendency to protect and that's exactly what she was doing. She needed to be objective about this.

"I'm not trying to protect that asshole," Haley snarled.

"Then give me one reason it's not him. Just one good reason why he's not doing this to pay you back for rejecting him"

Her breasts heaved under the tight white tee shirt she had slipped on after her bath. She was mad, that was evident. But there was something else, something more behind those jewel-toned eyes.

She shot him a glare. "I know it's not him. He broke up with me after I was kidnapped because he said I was ruined. Even my parents said I was damaged goods. He said he couldn't stay with me because I was beneath him because some other man had touched me." She curled her fingers into her palms as the words continued to spill. "Don't you see? To him, I'm not worth the trouble of being stalked."

CHAPTER 5

*H*aley quickly disappeared into the house.

Jayden stood paralyzed as his stomach heaved in disgust at what she'd just said.

They called her damaged goods. What kind of sadistic animals had she been raised by? Who the fuck does that to their own daughter, their own flesh and blood?

A growl tore from his mouth as his thoughts turned to the ex-boyfriend. If he ever came across that piece of shit, he was going to kill him and tear his fucking heart out with his teeth.

He hurried into the house and rounded the corner into the kitchen. It was empty. He strode toward the bedroom and stopped at the closed door. It was obvious that she wanted to be left alone.

Good thing he didn't take hints. He tried the knob. Locked.

Shit.

"Haley. Let me in."

"Go away, Jayden, I don't feel like talking." Her voice held a weariness that tugged within his chest.

"Haley, if you don't unlock this goddamn door right now, I'm kicking it in." No response.

"Have it your way." Jayden raised his hands above his head and grabbed the top of the doorframe. He jumped, kicking the door in as he growled. The door gave, breaking away from the frame and crashing to the floor.

Startled, Haley sat up on her knees in the middle of the bed and gasped.

Jayden planted himself at the foot of the bed in her direct line of vision. He wanted her to hear every fucking word of what he had to say.

"You are not damaged goods. I don't ever want to hear you say that again. Ever." His heart raced from the adrenaline that buzzed through his body as his breathing grew faster. His gaze drifted down to Haley's bare legs. She had changed clothes. Gone were the jeans and T-shirt. She was now wearing tight shorts that barely covered her ass and a short shirt that showed off her flat stomach.

She was practically naked.

Haley recovered her shock and propped her hands on her hips as she narrowed her gaze at him.

"Jayden, I'm not a child."

Hell no, not with a body like that. She was all woman.

"And I don't need you to try to make me feel better by some beautiful lies. I know what I am. What Were male is going to want me now?" She glared.

His nostrils flared as her feminine scent hit him. She smelled spicy and sweet, like pastries in a coffee shop.

Mine.

The word slipped from his brain into his veins, until it merged with his soul.

Mine.

A possessive growl left his body. He grabbed her by her arms and tugged her against him. The heat from her sweet nipples pressed into his chest scorching him with heat. Without thinking, he slammed his mouth down across hers, with a fiery heat that threatened to consume them both

Haley moaned and parted her lips under Jayden's demanding mouth.

She'd certainly been kissed before by her ex. But never like this. Never with such intensity and hunger. Since the kidnapping, she refused to let anyone touch her. She built up her walls by distancing herself from people and wearing baggy clothes. If she were invisible to guys, then no would notice her.

If no one noticed her, no one could hurt her.

Now, in this moment, with Jayden's mouth devouring hers, all she wanted to do was rip every stitch of clothing off their bodies. She wanted to feel his body against hers, flesh against flesh.

Jayden's hands slid down to cup her ass. She snaked her arms around his neck, their tongues sliding against and tasting each other in an erotic game of desire.

Lust ached in her lower stomach as she pressed against his rock-hard body to soothe her need. Her fingers found the bottom of his T-shirt and dipped underneath. She ran her hands up and down each silky, well-defined ab, eliciting a rugged groan from his lips.

She felt herself go wet. Her desire for him was so overwhelming it scorched her skin.

She reached for his T-shirt and tugged it up. He dipped his head, allowing her to strip the clothing off his body.

Their lips met again in a fevered kiss as his fingers slipped up her shirt.

The chirp of his cell phone made him tense. He growled as he reluctantly pulled out of her embrace.

Haley swallowed as he watched her with a thirst that had not been satisfied. He pulled out the phone, his gaze still locked on her.

"Hello." Jayden blinked and then looked away, running his hand through his blond hair.

Just like that, their moment was lost.

She eased back onto the bed, sitting on her heels. She pulled the comforter over her bare legs, and for the first time in a long time felt naked and vulnerable. She hated those feelings. She'd done everything in her power to keep them at bay. One kiss with Jayden had left her emotionally exposed. It was the one thing she'd sworn she'd never let happen again. It just cut too deep.

JAYDEN STEPPED over the broken bedroom door and grimaced. He wondered how Barrett would react to him damaging his property. Knowing the Were, he wouldn't be pleased. He walked out into the hallway deciding now was not the time to get all confessional with his Pack Master.

"I ran the envelope and letter for prints," Barrett said.

"You already got it?" Jayden frowned and looked at his watch. The delivery guy had picked up the package less than four hours ago.

"The delivery company knows I have top priority," Barrett groused.

Jayden wondered if the billion-dollar company was run by a werewolf as well.

"Both, the envelope and the letter were clean. They are running diagnostics on the paper to find out what stores in

Fayetteville sell that specific type."

Jayden nodded. Whoever had sent the letter knew enough not to leave any prints. "And then we can check to see if they have security cameras. Maybe they caught the perp on video."

"Or maybe someone remembers seeing him. I'll take whatever I can get."

Jayden didn't miss the deadly edge to Barrett's voice. Barrett was taking this personally, and for Haley's sake Jayden was glad. The stalker needed to be caught quickly.

"So you are going to tell me why you moved Haley into my house with you? Or do you want to play twenty questions?"

Jayden cringed and gritted his teeth. "It was no longer safe for her to be in the dorm. Barrett, the stalker left that note while I was in her dorm room. He was on the other side of the damn door and I didn't even sense it." Barrett was silent for a beat.

Jayden braced himself, ready to disobey Barrett's order of making Haley return to the dorm.

"You know the stalker is going to be pissed when he finds out Haley is gone. He's going to get more aggressive."

"Or maybe when he realizes she has a boyfriend, he will give up."

"Boyfriend? Is that what you are, Jayden?" Jayden didn't miss the edge to Barrett's voice.

"It's what I want him to think. If he thinks Haley is in a relationship and sees us together, then he might give up. And then Haley can finally get her life back. Damn man, she doesn't even eat in the cafeteria because she's too scared she'll run into him. I can't imagine having to live like that in college." "This whole situation is fucked up." Barrett sighed. "She can stay with you. But stay close and don't let her out of your sight for a second."

The line went dead.

Jayden shook his head. His Pack Master wasn't one for small talk.

"Was that Barrett?"

He knew she was standing behind him before she even spoke. He could still smell her arousal. He gritted his teeth, reminding himself that she was off limits.

"Yeah. There were no prints on the envelope." Jayden didn't turn around. He couldn't face her just yet. If he did, his resolve might falter

"Jayden..."

He flinched when she touched his arm. She quickly pulled away.

He turned. Hurt flickered across her face as she glanced away. His chest tightened. The last thing he ever wanted was to cause her more pain.

"Haley, I..." He took a step toward her.

She shook her head sharply and held up her hand. "I'm too tired to talk tonight. I'm going to bed."

He watched her disappear back into her bedroom. What the hell was wrong with him? He hadn't been interested in sex since October, since that night he'd been beaten half to death. But one moment alone with Haley and he was ready to fuck for hours.

Jayden pulled another bottle of beer from the fridge, making a mental note to buy something that wasn't alcoholic. He went from room to room, checking to make sure the windows and doors were secure before heading out to the deck.

Jayden flung himself in the lounge chair and took a long pull from the bottle. The icy liquid burned.

Though they were in the city, the stars were out tonight, brilliantly lighting up the backdrop of the midnight sky. It would have been perfect for a romantic dinner and a glass of wine.

"Who the hell am I kidding?" Jayden scrubbed his hand over his face. "I don't do romance."

For years, he'd been satisfied having sex without getting involved in a committed relationship. Up until last year. When Jayden had seen how Ava's love had changed Damon, he'd been hit with an unexpected dose of envy. Damon had never known what true love was until he met Ava. They had fallen in love and mated a short time later.

He'd never really thought about finding a mate. But when he saw how Damon seemed more content and happier than ever, Jayden wondered if it being mated wasn't such a bad idea after all.

Mate.

To willingly choose to forsake all other females and bind yourself to your mate until death was a difficult concept for him to grasp.

After that night of torture, he hadn't been able to bring himself to share a bed with a woman. Something had been stolen from him that night and he'd been struggling to reclaim the carefree life he'd once had.

Jayden took another drink and let his eyes drift shut.

Images of that night spilled out behind his closed lids. He remembered the stench of the room, stale urine and skunk, the typical telltale scent of red wolves. He'd gone into that filthy room in hopes of finding Haley. He'd been appalled when he found her, gagged and tied down to a filthy mattress that reeked of the rogue red wolf pack that had abducted her. She struggled with her bindings, trying to scream as a rogue wolf jumped on top of her and unzipped his pants.

Anger didn't begin to describe the emotion vibrating through his body at the scene. Jayden saw red, literally red, as he growled and snatched the wolf off Haley. Before the wolf knew what hit him, Jayden was there behind him, his hands placed strategically on the top and bottom of the wolf's head. He twisted, feeling the snap of the asshole's neck under his palms.

His rage had been so great that he hadn't stopped. He twisted until he almost ripped the rogue werewolf's head from his useless body. He would have pulled the guy's head clean off if those other three red wolves hadn't shown up and hit him in the head with a baseball bat.

Lights exploded from behind his eyes until he was blinded by the illumination. The blow had made him dizzy, unable to fight and defend himself. The next thing he knew he was stripped naked and tied up, hanging from the ceiling in a different room.

He grimaced against each slam of the bat against his body as the red wolf used his head as practice for his golf swing. Pain exploded throughout his head as he felt his eye socket shatter and his nose break in a snap. He could still taste the coppery acid as blood dripped into his mouth. He caught a blow against his ear, rattling his brain and making him momentarily lose all hearing on that side.

If Jayden had thought that was the extent of their torture, he had been wrong. Red wolves were violent and deadly, everyone thought they had become extinct by killing each other off. The Arkansas Pack had discovered there was still a small sect of red wolves, and they didn't follow Pack Law. And they certainly didn't play fair with the rules of war. Red wolves loved torture and got off on inflicting pain on others.

Jayden flinched as he recalled the feeling of cold wire being wrapped tightly around his genitals and thigh. Disgust and fear snaked up his spine thinking they were about to amputate his dick. He bit down hard, refusing to scream or to cry out. With every hit of the bat and kick in the ribs he'd only managed to groan out his pain. He wouldn't give them the satisfaction of screaming.

"Scream for me, Were." The red wolf's rancid breath hit his nose as he smiled menacingly close to Jayden.

"Fuck off." Jayden spat out another tooth he'd lost to the bat. He knew he could regenerate another tooth. If he got out alive.

"I bet I can make you scream. I bet I can make you scream like a little bitch." The red wolf stood and rubbed the frayed end of an extension cord against Jayden's bloody cheek. "I bet you're gonna scream now."

Jayden twisted in the air, trying his best to avoid the clamp being hooked to the wire around his penis. One guy wrapped him from behind, holding him still while the other snapped the clamp around the wire.

He twisted and turned and fought upside down and in midair trying to knock the clamp off. But he knew it was useless. The red Were held the frayed part of the extension cord in front of his face, taunting him with the pain that was coming.

Jayden watched wide-eyed as the other Were picked up the other end of the extension cord and held it toward the outlet.

"Did you think you could stop us from having that female? She's ours now, and we're gonna take turns using that tight little body until that pussy is good and sore." The Were grabbed his crotch and shoved it in Jayden's face. Jayden gagged at the rancid smell.

"That little piece of tail in there is gonna be begging for us to pound her hard." Both red Weres laughed. "But first, I wanna hear you scream." Jayden bit back a growl. The sooner he screamed the sooner they would get to Haley. He couldn't let that happen.

"Go fuck yourself," he sneered.

"Light him up!" The red Were growled.

Jayden had experienced broken bones, bruised internal organs, and even stab wounds during fights he'd gotten into over the years.

Nothing would have prepared him for what came next. With the extension cord plugged into the outlet, the Were touched the frayed end to the wire around his penis.

Hot, angry pain spread from his dick to his balls before traveling throughout his entire body, making all his muscles contract uncontrollably. He wanted to scream, to cry out, but the muscles in his cheek clamped down, refusing to let the pain out as electricity racked his body. Pain, excruciating pain, beyond anything he'd every experienced, licked through every muscle and organ in his body until he was sure his heart would stop. He couldn't even breathe.

If the electricity didn't stop his heart, he was going to die from lack of oxygen.

Jayden eyes popped open and he looked around. He was in Fayetteville, far from Louisiana. He sucked in deep breaths, the nightmare he'd relived much too vivid.

He swiped a hand across his sweaty brow and sat up in the Adirondack chair. Night had fallen and the only light came from the neighbor's back porch illuminating the back yard.

In the end, he had held out. He hadn't screamed when they had tortured him. Not once. In between shock treatments he had tried to catch his breath so he wouldn't suffocate with the next round of electrocution.

He must have passed out from lack of oxygen because the next thing he remembered was waking up tied to a chair and hearing Ava's voice. She had on a little red riding hood stripper costume and was trying to get him out of that strip club where he was tied to a chair.

He discovered later that night that Haley had gotten out and was safe. That was all he had to hear before he passed out as the medical Werewolf Guardians worked on his broken body.

He never told anyone about the shock torture he had endured. He hadn't even told Barrett when he came to visit him in the infirmary.

It wasn't anyone's business. And he wanted to leave it buried in the past. The funny thing about burying shit was that it had a tendency to sprout roots and want to push itself back up through the dirt like a weed.

In the end it hadn't mattered. He hadn't managed to save Haley from being raped.

Jayden stood and headed back inside. He tossed his glass beer bottle in the garbage can as he passed through the kitchen.

He had tried to take advantage of her just minutes ago while she was vulnerable. That didn't make him any better than those rogue red Weres

He knew without a doubt that there was something wrong deep inside of him. Something that could never be fixed.

Haley looked up from sipping her hot coffee at the kitchen table as Jayden walked into the room. Dressed in jeans and a tight fitting T-shirt, his sandy blonde hair still damp from his shower, he looked like every red-blooded girl's fantasy. Her heart fluttered against her chest and she couldn't tear her gaze away. It wasn't fair that he was so gorgeous without even trying, while she'd just spend half an hour trying to style her hair.

"You're up early." Jayden looked at his military style watch before meeting her gaze. "It's only six thirty."

"I wanted to look over my notes before class." Haley swallowed.

Jayden nodded and poured himself a cup of coffee. She waited to see if he was going to add cream. He didn't. Figured. He liked his coffee manly, not with French vanilla creamer and sugar like she preferred.

He frowned at her plate "Is that all you're going to eat?"

She glanced down at her half-eaten toast. "Yeah."

Jayden shook his head. "Get your stuff. We'll go grab a real breakfast."

"But I need to look over my notes."

"Bring them. You'll have time to look over them after you eat a real meal. You've lost weight and you need a good breakfast before your test."

She stared at him. How did he know that she had lost weight? After the notes arrived she'd lost her appetite. When she did manage to eat, it wasn't much.

She walked into the bedroom and sat on the bed, tucking her textbooks into her backpack.

She grabbed her cell phone and tucked it in her jeans pocket and headed for the door. The mirror on the wall caught her attention and she jerked to a stop, looking at her appearance.

She had chosen the silky peach top that dipped slightly between her breasts and jeans that weren't so baggy. They weren't tight-fitting, but they still hung lower on her hips and hugged her curves better than the bigger jeans she usually wore.

She had even put on some eye shadow and lip gloss. The

shadows under her eyes were still there, but lighter thanks to a good night's sleep. She felt lighter too.

Was it because of Jayden?

"You ready?" Jayden called out from the kitchen.

She grinned at her reflection. Was she ready?

Hell, yeah.

JAYDEN LEANED BACK in the booth of the busy little café and studied Haley over his coffee as she read over her notes before their breakfast arrived.

He nearly had a coronary when he walked into the kitchen and saw her in those low rise jeans and peach shirt that flowed over her breasts.

She was a natural beauty with her full lips and a complexion that didn't need any makeup. Her full lips shone with that cherry lip gloss she'd put on. He knew it was cherry because he could smell it.

And he wanted to lick it off.

She had been trying to hide herself behind those baggy clothes. But today she wasn't. She was even walking with her head up, instead of watching the ground.

It was enough to make him smile.

Haley looked up from her notes. A slow grin spread across her face and Jayden almost choked on his coffee as he felt his body respond.

"What are you smiling at?" She cocked her head. "Do I have something on my face?"

"What? No." He cleared his throat as he shifted his weight in the booth. His jeans were growing tighter by the second "I was just noticing the change in your wardrobe."

She chuckled. "I didn't think it was such a big change. I wore jeans yesterday."

"Jeans that are much too big. Plus the ugly sweatshirt."

"Hey! No making fun of the university. That will get your ass kicked." She grinned.

"Whatever." Jayden grinned and looked away, both shocked and pleased at how good it felt to sit with her and share a meal. Made him feel almost alive again.

"So what's up with your wardrobe?" She pointed the end of her pencil at his shirt.

He jerked his head towards her. "What do you mean?"

"I've noticed all you ever wear are T-shirts."

"So?"

"From that store in the mall." She arched her brow.

Jayden crossed his arms and frowned. "What's wrong with that?"

"Is that the official uniform for being a Guardian?"

"No." He glanced down at his bright blue shirt. "It's just what I wear when I'm not working. Plus I thought I was blending into the college crowd."

Haley bit her lip and nodded before looking back down at her textbook.

"Are you trying to tell me I need to get some different clothes? Are you sure you're not trying to turn me into your guinea pig for some class project for your fashion course?"

She rolled her eyes. "Look, you've got a great body. You need to dress it accordingly."

He fought a grin, pleased way too much that she liked his body. "Tell me, how would you dress me?"

He watched her cock her head and study him. It made him feel a little like a piece of meat.

"You need more button-up shirts that are tailored to fit you. Your jeans fit fine, but you should go with a darker wash with some whiskering effect on the front. If it were winter I'd tell you to wear scarves and layer them into your wardrobe. But we are going into spring, which will quickly turn into summer, so you could wear more shirts with patterns versus solid colors. And if you do go with a solid, you need to do softer colors. Not bright-colored T-shirts."

She crossed her arms and smiled, waiting for his rebuttal.

"Button-up shirts are too dressy and scarves are for girls. I don't wear patterned shirts because they remind me of Granny's muumuus," he snarled.

"Okay." Haley shrugged, took a sip of coffee and went back to studying.

He fidgeted in his seat until he couldn't take it anymore. "Are you trying to insinuate that I don't look good in my clothes?" He'd never had a woman complain before. Hell, they were always trying to take his clothes off, not put clothes on him.

Haley set her coffee down. "Jayden, would you dress a lingerie model in granny panties and an oversized bra?" She shook her head. "No, you'd dress her in the hottest lingerie that would best show off her body."

He didn't know if he should be offended or complimented. He cocked his head, trying to figure her out.

He leaned forward, his elbows on the table. Her breath hitched ever so slightly in her slender throat and he could see the pulse jumping at the base of her neck. Her pupils dilated. Pleasure streaked through his body hard and fast at her obvious arousal.

He let his lips curve into a slow grin. "Okay, Haley. I'm willing to be your little experiment. I'll let you strip me down and dress me however you want."

Her eyelids drifted over her eyes as her lips parted. He loved seeing that reaction.

"How about we make a deal?"

"What kind of deal?" Her raspy voice made his dick throb.

"I'll let you take me shopping for clothes and let you

change my wardrobe however you like." He shrugged. "I'll even pay for everything."

"What do you want in return?"

"In return, you've got to do something for me." He let his gaze dip down to that pulse in her neck that seemed to pick up speed at his proposal.

"What do you want me to do?"

That was a loaded question. There was a lot he wanted her to do and it all involved her being naked.

"I want you to let me give you the college experience that you've been missing. Everything that you've missed out on, everything that you've been warned not to do. I want you to agree to do whatever I say."

Haley stared at him for a few beats, as if considering his proposal.

Any other woman would have been putty in his hands.

But not Haley.

She was different. She had a mind of her own.

Haley eased back in her seat and met his gaze. "Okay, on one condition. You can't refuse what I pick out for you. You have to buy it and wear it."

"Okay." He shrugged and gave her an easy grin.

She stuck out her hand and smiled. He took her hand in his and shook, holding on to her hand a second too long.

He leaned closer.

"Remember, Haley, a deal's a deal. There's no going back now."

JAYDEN WALKED Haley to each one of her classes and stood watch just outside the door. He managed to pass the time researching stalkers on his cell phone. He discovered that all stalkers were not the same. There were actually different types. Haley's stalker resembled what they called a rejected suitor.

One person fit that description.

The ex-boyfriend.

He lifted his head as the doors to the classroom swung opened and students poured out into the hallway like ants. He ignored the flirty looks the girls were shooting him and instead kept his gaze on Haley as she headed toward him, her head high and a smile on her lips. A girl walking beside her touched her arm and Haley turned. She said something and they both laughed.

His heart tugged in his chest and he couldn't tear his eyes off her.

Neither could the other males in the hallway.

Jayden frowned, watching a guy slide up beside her and ask her a question. His gut burned. Jayden started moving closer to her.

Haley replied to whatever the dude has said to her and shook her head before looking back at Jayden and smiling.

He wasted no time wading through the throng of people to get to her.

"How was class?" he asked, sticking his hands in his jeans pockets. He realized he was standing close, but he couldn't seem to make himself step back.

"It was good." Haley smiled and slung her backpack across her shoulders.

"I got it." He took her backpack and slung it across his shoulder. "Is that your last class for the day?" He slowed his pace adjusting to her stride as they walked out of the building and toward the direction of his car.

"Yep. She stuck her hands in the back pocket of her jeans. Her breasts strained against the thin material of her shirt. A couple of guys passed by, their gaze zeroed in on Haley's chest. Jayden let out a growl. The guys hurried away.

"So what did you do all day?" She looked up at him. "I'm sure you were bored to death."

"Actually I was looking up Fayetteville's upcoming activities." He grinned. No need for her to know about his

stalker research. "For your college experience."

"Oh yeah. How could I forget?" She laughed.

"Haley!"

Jayden followed Haley's gaze to her roommate, Dana, who was running across campus toward them. He'd seen Dana around Little Rock and knew she had a penchant for trying to catch a sneak peek of the Guardians while they were working out or trying to get dressed. Truth be told, she was going to get herself in a whole lot of trouble with that kind of behavior.

"Hey." Dana frowned at Haley and then gave Jayden a surprised look.

"Hi, Dana." Haley frowned and shifted her weight. "I'm sorry I moved out in such a hurry…"

Dana crossed her arms and gave her a scowl. "You didn't even wait until I got back to the dorm. You could have at least told me face-to-face." She looked over at Jayden and then back at Haley.

"Yeah, I know. It all happened very quickly and well…" Jayden pulled Haley into his arms.

"Sorry, Dana. It's my fault. I realized I couldn't be away from Haley another day." Jayden looked down into Haley's surprised expression and covered her lips in a blazing hot kiss.

*J*ayden's warm lips covered hers and she opened her mouth, welcoming him to taste her. He took the invitation and slipped his hot tongue inside her willing mouth. Her fingertips gripped his narrow waist, momentarily forgetting Dana was standing there. She pressed closer, wanting to crawl inside him until they were one.

Slowly he pulled away, leaving her breathless and startled at her own quick reaction. His blue eyes bored into hers, searing her with a look of lust that made her shiver despite the warmth of the spring day.

"Wow. I had no idea you guys were dating." Dana grinned.

Still dizzy from Jayden's kiss, Haley glanced at her friend and murmured, "Yeah, me either." Her nerve endings tingled from the contact of the kiss.

She tried to step back to clear her head, but Jayden didn't release his hold. He slipped his hand around her waist and pulled her in front of him, pressing her back into his chest. He nuzzled her neck. She had to fight to keep her eyes from fluttering shut.

"You sure know how to keep a secret, Haley. I should be mad that you didn't at least tell me." A streak of pain flashed in Dana's eyes.

"I'm sorry, Dana. I didn't mean to keep anything from you." She hated that she'd betrayed her friend. Dana had been a good friend to her since she moved here and she would never intentionally hurt her. But most of all she hated lying to Dana. "It's my fault, actually." Jayden cleared his throat. "I didn't really want anyone to know how involved we were. It might cause some unwanted talk about the difference in our ages"

Dana's eyes narrowed as she looked between them. "Surely you can't be that much older than Haley? What are you, twenty five?"

Haley snorted.

Jayden squeezed her tight. "Something like that."

"You guys look so cute together." Dana's expression softened as she looked between them.

"Really?" Haley looked up at Jayden.

"Yeah, like Ken and Barbie," Dana said brightly. "I don't look like Ken," Jayden groused.

"Well, like a surfer Ken, you know, with all your bright-colored T-shirts."

Haley bit the inside of her cheek. She didn't have to look at Jayden's face to see he was glaring.

"Well, I'm heading to the library to study. I'm supposed to have dinner with my sweetie tonight. You two should come."

Haley shook her head. "I don't think Mark would appreciate us busting in on his romantic dinner for two. Besides, it sounds like he is trying to make you and your relationship a priority."

Dana shot them a sheepish look. "Or it might have something to do with him catching me flirting with a certain professor of his."

"Dana!" Haley's mouth dropped open.

Dana frowned. "What? I was trying to see if Mark would even notice. He's been so busy with his classes lately."

"And did he notice?"

"Dana grinned. "Oh, yeah. Not only is he taking me out to dinner, he is insisting that I spend the night at his apartment. Which has never happened."

"You've never spent the night at your boyfriend's apartment?" Jayden asked over Haley's shoulder.

"No." Dana pouted. "He's always telling me that he has to study and that when I'm over there he can't concentrate because I distract him too much."

"Sounds like a nice problem for a guy to have." Jayden laughed.

"I guess you would know since you two are living together." Dana glanced down at her cell phone in her hand. "I need to go if I'm going to study before I get ready for my date. Maybe we can all do something together this weekend?"

Haley shivered as she forced a smile to her lips. She wasn't sure if she was ready to be out in public with someone still stalking her.

"Let me see what we have planned and we'll get back with you," Jayden answered for her.

"Sounds good." Dana gave Haley a wink before making her way back to the dorm.

Haley waited for Jayden to release her since Dana was out of sight, but he didn't.

"So how much homework do you have?" His breath tickled her ear sending butterflies fluttering around her stomach.

Slowly she shook her head trying to calm her racing

heart. Her body warmed under the embrace of his protective body. "I don't have any homework and my next test is Monday."

"So you're free?"

"Pretty much." She tried to catch her breath. She was pretty sure he could feel her heart racing. She sucked in a deep breath and concentrated on not grinding her butt against his crotch.

"Good." He released his hold.

She forced herself to step away. She needed to get used to letting him go. Jayden was here on a job, not for anything else.

To him, she was just a mission.

She rubbed her hand across her chest, easing the tiny ache that found its way into her heart.

She knew Jayden would leave just like her family had. She wasn't going to let it devastate her like before. She didn't have to be a victim. She could choose to look at this short time with Jayden as an opportunity, an opportunity to learn how to be herself again and to live.

Lifting her chin, she turned and faced him. He was gorgeous standing there, all cut muscles, blue eyes and blonde hair, like something out of a surfer magazine.

"I'm not sure I like that look in your eye," Jayden teased.

"I'm thinking how I want to redo you." Not that it mattered.

He could wear a potato sack and still look hot.

"Why does that scare me?" Jayden reached out and took her hand as they headed towards the parking lot.

Her heart tugged at the warmth of their hands. She shook her head and quickly willed her body to stop being such an idiot every time he touched her.

"Don't be scared. I happen to think you would look really

good in pink." She gave him a cheery smile as he laced his fingers through hers.

Jayden halted midstride. "Pink."

Haley gave him an innocent look. She tried not to laugh at the horrified expression on his face.

"We did make a deal. And there's no going back on a deal."

AFTER DINING on burgers and fries at the local hole in the wall restaurant, Jayden drove to the mall. They made their way into the department store. Haley's face lit up with excitement.

He took her hand in his, telling himself it was for show, pretending to be a couple so he wouldn't blow his cover. He also had told himself that same lie when he had kissed her in front of Dana.

He knew better. He'd kissed her because he wanted the rest of the world to know who she belonged to. He'd kissed her because all day he'd suffered through watching all those college assholes gawk at her with lust. He'd kissed her because he needed it more than his next breath.

"Jayden?"

He shook his head, forcing his thoughts under control. "Yeah?'

"I asked what size jeans you wear." She glanced back at the display. Her gaze was glued to the mannequin wearing dark denim jeans the color of midnight.

"I thought you said my jeans were fine." He glanced down at his favorite denims. He'd had them forever and they fit him just right

"Come, Jayden, let me play." She stepped up to him,

pressing her palms to his chest, while her full lips curved into a sexy pout.

His nostrils flared. On instinct, he cupped the back of her head and swiped his thumb across her bottom lip. "Be careful,

Sweetheart. I don't play gentle."

"Neither do I." Her eyes flared with lust.

He was trying to warn her away from him. But she wasn't having it. His shy little college girl wasn't backing down from him.

His cock hardened behind his zipper, making his jeans uncomfortably tight. His heartbeat drummed in his chest and he could feel it all the way to his balls.

Jayden slammed his eyes shut and gritted his teeth.

"What's wrong?"

He opened his eyes and scowled. "I'm trying to get myself under control." Did she have no idea what she did to him?

"And what exactly do I do?"

He pulled her against him. Her eyes grew wide as his cock pressed into her stomach. A blush stole across her face.

Then that little minx did the unexpected. Instead of stepping back, Haley reached up on her tiptoes and sucked his earlobe into her hot little mouth.

"Fuck, Haley," he growled as lust slammed into his stomach so violently he considered taking her right there against the wall.

She didn't even have the courtesy to look sorry. Instead, she laughed.

Taking a step back, she grabbed his hand. "Come on, let's go in here. I'm sure once you start trying on clothes you'll lose your erection."

Now it was his turn to look shocked.

She looked across her shoulder and grinned. "Maybe I'll

help you out and put some pink on you. I'm sure you'll lose your hard-on then.

"Are you sure you don't want me to carry anything?" Haley cut her eyes at Jayden as they walked out of the mall and into the parking lot. The slight breeze drifted across her, chilling her skin.

"No, I got it." Jayden shook his head as he carried three bags in each hand with ease.

"Are you still pouting?"

"I don't pout," he groused.

"Okay." Haley nodded her head, not believing him for a second. "So are you still upset about me dressing you up?" Jayden shot her a glare. She couldn't help but laugh.

"That shirt looked really good on you. I don't see what the big deal is." When he'd walked out of the dressing room, all she wanted to do was lick him from head to toe.

"I told you I don't wear pink."

"It's not pink, it's coral." And he looked hot in it.

"It looks a hell of lot like pink to me. Can you imagine what the other Guardians would say if they see that on me?" He grimaced.

"Then don't wear it around them. " She shrugged. She'd been around the Guardians enough in Arkansas to know they wore jeans and leather and rode Harleys. To humans, they looked a like a biker gang.

"I don't go anywhere but to work, Haley." He shrugged. "It's not like I'll have a place to wear it or any of this other stuff."

She pasted a smile on and forced the next words out. "Then wear it when you go on a date."

His gaze hardened before he glanced away. The mood between them shifted.

"It's been a while since I had a date."

She frowned.

That's not what she had heard. In fact, Dana was constantly talking about how many women Jayden had gone through. From his reputation, he was insatiable in bed.

"I don't think a week constitutes a long time." She elbowed him, trying to lighten his mood.

Jayden stopped and faced her, his expression grim. "The last time I took a woman out on a date was over six months ago."

Haley's smile slipped. Her mind quickly calculated the date and she realized that would have been around the time she had been abducted.

"Besides, I don't date, Haley. I hook up with women." His eyes narrowed, driving the point home.

"Okay." She knew this about him already. She didn't expect him to be celibate, for heaven's sake.

He shook his head and looked away, frustration creasing his brow. "I shouldn't have bought this. It's just a waste of money."

Haley's chest ached as self-doubt crept through her heart. She dropped her head. She didn't want to push Jayden to do something he didn't want to do. Heaviness settled across her shoulders like a shroud of guilt.

She dug out her cell phone and pulled up her inspiration app. It had been her go-to since she'd moved to Arkansas and felt abandoned by everyone that had ever mattered. She knew she was going to have to find a life on her own now and she was determined to have the life she wanted. This time she was doing it on her terms.

"Happiness is a choice that requires effort at times"—Aeschylus.

She wasn't sure who the hell Aeschylus was, but he hit the nail on the head.

Sucking in a deep breath, she slipped her phone back in her purse and looked at Jayden. "If you really think it's a waste then take it back." She grabbed his keys out of his jean pocket. "I'll wait in the car."

HE WAS A DICKHEAD.

He'd seen the hurt in her eyes.

"Haley, wait." He quickened his steps to catch up to Haley as she stomped away. He hadn't meant to hurt her feelings.

"Haley, wait." He jogged around in front of her blocking her path. "I'm sorry. I didn't mean to hurt your feelings. You put a lot of effort into making me look good. I didn't mean to dismiss that."

She crossed her arms and glared at him, as her foot tapped against the asphalt.

"Would it make you feel better if you told me to fuck off?"

"Maybe." *Tap, tap, tap.* She held his gaze.

"What I said came out wrong." He was able to talk a female out of her panties, but trying to apologize was more painful than listening to his Granny talk about sex toys.

"How's that?" She continued the incessant tapping of her foot against the ground.

"I actually like the clothes. I think you really did a good job picking stuff out." He swallowed. Why the hell was this so hard?

She stood there in silence.

"Look, I don't date. I haven't for a very long time." He blew out a breath.

"And I haven't had a date in over six months either, but it's not like I've written off ever finding someone, or given up dating." She shrugged. "Maybe you've just gotten picky. Maybe what you used to like isn't what you want anymore."

What he wanted was her. Naked and in his bed with his

face between her sweet thighs. Jayden's breathing increased as his body hardened with overwhelming lust.

"That's not all of it."

"Then what is it?" She cocked her head, waiting for an answer. For someone who'd been stalked for months she certainly wasn't scared of him.

"I don't date because I…" His voice trailed off, the words refusing to come out. A cold sweat popped across his skin as his thoughts turned to that night of torture.

"You don't owe me an explanation, Jayden. You don't owe me anything." Haley stepped around him.

He stood there for a second, trying to shove the memories away and lock them down.

He shook his head and followed after her. He caught up to her as he stood at the hood of the Mustang.

"Look, I…" The words trailed off as he met her pale face and wide eyes.

Jayden followed Haley's frozen stare. On the windshield stuck under the wiper was an envelope with Haley's name sprawled across the top.

"Shit." He dropped the bags and reached in his boot for the concealed gun he always carried. He sandwiched Haley between him and the pickup truck parked next to him.

"Get down." Jayden searched the parking lot, hoping to catch a glance of the stalker. He only spotted one elderly couple getting out of the car and heading inside.

Squatting down in front of her, he met her scared gaze and caressed her cheek. "Are you okay?"

She looked from him to his hand. "You have a gun."

"Yeah."

"You didn't tell me you had a gun." She trembled as her eyes widened.

"You didn't ask." He quickly checked his car, making sure

it was safe from explosives before unlocking the door. If someone had tried to set an explosive or tried to place a tracking device on the Mustang, the car would have alerted him via his phone. It was one of the many perks for working with Barrett and his Guardians. They always had the latest technology, far beyond what the public had access to.

"Let's get the hell out of here." He helped Haley into the front seat and buckled her in before going to his side.

"Don't forget your bags," she murmured as he opened the car door.

Jayden growled. He didn't give two shits about the clothes but thought it was better not to argue with her. He was just relieved she wasn't in shock. For a second he thought she was going to pass out on him.

After shoving the bags in the backseat and swiping the envelope off the windshield, he got in and peeled out of the parking lot. He turned on the street headed out of town.

"Where are we going?'

"We are going the long way home. Just to make sure we are not being followed." He cast a glance at her.

She nodded and clenched her purse like a shield to her chest. Her gaze was glued to the envelope sitting on the console. She angled her body away from the offending paper, scared to even touch it

"You're safe. I'm not going to let him get you." Jayden put the envelope on the backseat and out of her line of sight. He reached for her hand. Her cold fingers tightened around his.

He would protect her no matter what.

"I know, Jayden." She met his gaze, humbling him with her utter trust in him.

This time he wouldn't let her down.

This time he would kill before he would let harm come to her.

"He left the note on my fucking car, Barrett." Jayden glared across the back deck of the house as he fought to keep his wolf side under control. Anger surged through his veins and he wanted nothing more than to shift so he could run all this hatred off.

"How's Haley?" Barrett asked.

"She's shook up. She wanted to know what the envelope said. I think she's pretty pissed that I wouldn't let her read it." Jayden forked his fingers through his hair. "She's in bed now, asleep."

"Good call. She doesn't need to know what it says. All it does is feed the stalker's ego and his need for attention." Jayden could hear the tap of Barrett's fingertips on his keyboard. "What did the note say?"

Jayden growled as he recited the vile words. *"I'm coming for you, Haley. I'm coming to take you to our perfect paradise where no one can find us. I'm going to tie you up and fuck you until you scream my name."* That's not all. Put some gloves on before you open the envelope."

"I doubt he'll leave finger prints."

"That's not why you need the gloves. The motherfucker jacked off on the letter." Jayden had smelled the stench of semen the second he reached for it. But he said nothing, not wanting to freak Haley out any more than she already was. She didn't say anything, but he couldn't help but wonder if she smelled it too.

"Sick fuck." Barrett's tapping stopped.

"On the bright side you have your DNA."

"I would have preferred to get a DNA sample another way," Barrett said dryly.

"No shit." Jayden blew out a breath. "Any word on the ex-boyfriend?"

"He has made no phone calls anywhere in Arkansas and he's not received any from Arkansas. He seems to be busy dating his new girlfriend from LSU, whom he started dating a week after Haley was rescued. Total douche bag."

If Jayden ever laid eyes on that asshole, he was going to beat the shit out of that prick.

"Have you notice anyone showing Haley attention when she's out and about on campus?"

"You're kidding, right? Half the male population can't keep their fucking eyes in their head when she walks by. I saw one dude get slapped by his girlfriend when she caught him staring at Haley's ass." Jayden scowled. If the girlfriend hadn't slapped him, Jayden would have punched him the fuck out.

Barrett snorted.

"What?"

"You're sounding a little green there, Jayden."

"Are you trying to insinuate something?" Jayden gritted his teeth.

"No. I'm saying you sound like a jealous mate, flat out."

"I'm just here doing my job. That's all." Jayden shook his head. What did Barrett know about it, anyway?

"Famous last words. Damon said the same damn thing about Ava."

"This situation is different. I'm different." Jayden clenched his jaw, irritated that Barrett would even try to compare him with Damon. After all the bullshit that Damon had gone through the male deserved someone like Ava.

Haley deserved someone better than him.

"I'll call you if he gets a match on the DNA. Until, then, keep Haley safe." Barrett disconnected.

FRUSTRATED, Haley bolted up in bed and glared at the neon numbers on the clock.

1:00 a.m. What the hell? She hadn't even slept one damn hour. She was going to be exhausted in the morning.

Every time she closed her eyes, she saw that semen-coated note, taunting her with whatever hidden evil message was stuck inside its white walls. The fact that Jayden wouldn't let her read what was on it made it even worse. Since they'd gotten home that's all she could think about.

"Screw this." She climbed out of the bed and padded over to the wall to turn the light on. Snatching her pillow and a blanket off the bed, she headed for the living room. She flung herself on the couch and reached for the remote.

"Maybe some mindless entertainment will lull me to sleep."

"What are you doing up?" Jayden stood in the doorway, bare chest with his jeans hanging low on his lean hips. He rubbed his hand across his muscled chest as he leaned against the doorframe waiting for her answer.

Haley's mouth dropped open as her gaze wandered down his finely chiseled chest. He didn't have six pack abs; he had a twelve pack.

"I can't sleep." She forced her eyes to meet his. Hopefully it was dark enough that he didn't catch her gawking at his half-nude body. "Did I wake you?"

"I was finishing up some research on the Internet. I was just getting ready to go to bed." He crossed his arms over his massive chest. His muscles rippled under the motion in a sexy yet dangerous way.

"Okay. Good night. I'll see you in the morning." She aimed the remote at the TV and clicked.

"You really need to try to sleep. You've got class tomorrow." His deep voice drifted over her.

"I know. It's just…" She cringed, ashamed that she felt so

helpless. "Every time I close my eyes I see that envelope. And I feel like he's here, watching me."

His bare feet on the hardwood floor made no sound as he walked towards her. The chill she felt earlier was now gone, and she shifted on the couch.

Jayden sat on the coffee table blocking her view of the infomercial casting lights against the walls in the dark.

"He doesn't know that you are here. The house is secure.

You're safe, Haley."

"I know that. My head knows that. But my imagination didn't get the memo." She let out a frustrated laugh.

He stood and held out his hand. "Come on."

"I told you I can't sleep."

Jayden took her hand and pulled her up with him. Her heart sped up at his touch. She couldn't make herself to pull away. His touch soothed her, made her feel safe and protected. Made her feel wanted.

"You're not sleeping in your bed." He tugged her down the hall and stopped at his bedroom door. "You're sleeping in mine."

Warmth spread from her chest down between her thighs as she stared at the bed where he'd been sleeping. She looked from the bed back to him.

"What?" Surely she had misunderstood him. He had pulled away from her only a few hours ago and now he was offering an invitation to sleep in his bed. "You're sleeping in my bed."

"Where are you going to sleep?" She frowned, trying to make her brain compute as her breathing turning to a soft pant.

"Beside you." His deep voice sent shivers of pleasure shooting across her skin.

"I just thought you would be able to relax knowing I was there to keep you safe." He shrugged.

Just like that, her heart melted like a hot caramel at his kind gesture.

"It's just sleeping, Haley." He rubbed the back of his neck, looking a little uncomfortable.

He'd probably never had to ask a woman to sleep in his bed before. They were probably all breaking their necks to jump right in.

"I know, Jayden. I trust you." She touched his arm as she met his intense blue-eyed gaze. A ghost of a smile hovered on his lips and he nodded once.

Walking to the bed, he tugged the covers down and waited for her to crawl in. He started to unbutton his jeans and then froze.

"What's wrong?"

"I don't wear underwear." A faint blush stole across his cheeks.

"To bed?" Haley swallowed. The thought of Jayden sleeping nude had her blood heating like a hot July summer. What would one night with him, wrapped in his arms, be like?

"Ever." Jayden grumbled as went to the dresser and pulled out some basketball shorts before heading for the bathroom.

Haley snuggled down into the warm covers. She inhaled deeply, letting Jayden's masculine scent wash over her.

Minutes later she felt Jayden slide into bed behind her. Unfortunately he made no move toward her but kept to his side of the bed. If she weren't so tired it would have hurt her feelings. But not tonight. Her disappointment soon gave way to sleep as her eyes drifted shut.

JAYDEN OPENED his eyes just as the first light of dawn spilled gently through the blinds, casting the room in a soft glow.

He knew the second he opened his eyes what he would find. Haley snuggled against his chest, her body pressed against every angle of his frame and his arms wrapped around her. Her scent drifted up to him and heated his body.

He had waited until she fell asleep before he scooted closer. He didn't touch her but settled for watching as she finally rested peacefully and without a care in the world. Without worrying if her stalker was right around the corner, waiting for his opportunity to grab her.

Jayden tightened his hold on her, fighting to keep the negative thoughts out of his head of what could happen if the stalker found Haley. He wouldn't let that happen, not this time.

He was almost asleep when he felt her snuggle against him last night seeking out his warmth. He had been helpless not to touch her. So he pulled her into his arms, settling her against him before going back to sleep himself.

Something had shifted inside him, something changed and made him feel like he wasn't himself. He felt more peace and comfortable when he was with Haley than he had in a while.

It scared the hell out of him.

They couldn't go down this road. There was no future for them. She deserved to be with a male who was worthy of her.

And that male wasn't Jayden

But right now, he would hold onto her and pretend.

Right now, he couldn't let her go. He knew the time was drawing near when he wouldn't have that choice.

The time would come when she found out about him and she would be the one to walk away.

Haley knew it was morning by the light trying to sneak in behind her closed eyes. She didn't want to move. If she moved, the moment would be gone. She wanted to stay right where she was, snuggled in Jayden's arms.

When she first realized she had her leg draped over his and was wrapped around him she had almost pulled away, embarrassed at how she had ended up like that during the night.

She knew that if Jayden realized she was awake he would pull away. So she faked it and pretended to be asleep, just to enjoy the feel of his body for a few minutes longer.

His delicious heat sunk into her skin, warming her. Her nipples hardened, and she knew he could probably feel them against his bare chest through the thin material of her shirt. Her hand rested low on his steely abs and her fingers itched to trace each deep groove of muscle lower until she was holding him in her hand.

Her stomach tugged with lust at the mental image of Jayden lying naked and letting her explore his body with her hand and her mouth and her tongue.

He moved under her hands as he took a deep breath. She knew he was awake. Still she stayed still, eyes closed, with her dreams clasped in her head.

Maybe if she believed hard enough she'd get her wish. After all, everyone deserved to get at least one wish in their life. God knows all her other wishes had long been forgotten.

Maybe her wishes didn't come true because she had always hoped someone would grant them to her. Look how that turned out.

No, if she wanted something, she was going to have to reach out and take it herself.

With her body getting warmer by the second and lust licking deep in her stomach, Haley trailed her hand down Jayden's stomach until she reached the waistband of his shorts.

Her fingertips slid behind the elastic and she wrapped her hand around Jayden's rock hard erection.

CHAPTER 7

*J*ayden had been trying his damnedest to feign sleep. But with Haley's tempting body pressed against his like a second skin, he couldn't control his sex-starved body. His body ached with lust as his cock hardened to the point of pain.

He was in dangerous territory where she was concerned, yet he still couldn't make his arms release her. Instead, he pulled her closer.

He knew the second she was awake. Her breathing increased as she stirred against him, her body coming to life. It was like electricity, sparking between their bodies, burning him with a passion so sweet it hurt.

The second he felt the brush of her hand against his abs he expected her to pull away. He wasn't expecting her to slide her hand down into his shorts and wrap her fingers around his aching cock.

"Haley, what are you doing?" Jayden groaned out between clenched teeth as her hand tightened around his shaft and slowly stroked.

"If you have to ask, then I'm doing it wrong." She slid her

hand up to the tip. Her thumb circled the head before she slid her hand back down to the base.

"Haley…" She was going to fucking kill him with pleasure. He squeezed his eyes shut and tried to focus on anything but her talented hand.

She lifted her head and met his gaze. She was beautiful, sleepy eyes and kissable lips. All he could think about was getting her naked and burying himself in her hot little body.

"Am I hurting you?" She gave him a hard squeeze.

He jerked his hips upward and groaned.

"Fuck, no." Jayden closed his hand over hers, searching her face for any hesitation, any reason why they should stop.

"This isn't a good idea." He forced the words past his lips and rose up on his elbow.

"Let me, Jayden. Just for a little bit." She glanced at the clock. "It's not like we have time to do much else." He let his head hit the pillow.

She smiled and reached for the sheet to pull it down. He grabbed the covers.

"Don't pull the sheet down." He swallowed as his heart thudded in his chest. A thin sheen of sweat broke out across his body.

"Okay." She frowned but didn't ask any questions. Leaving the sheet in place, she laid her head against his shoulder and met his gaze. She slid her hand under the sheet and gripped his cock again.

"Harder, like this." Jayden covered her hand with his and squeezed, showing her how hard he like it.

She tightened her grip.

"Shit." He let go of her hand and squeezed his eyes shut, the pleasure too intense to bear.

Her lips slanted over his and suddenly she was kissing him, snaking that sweet tongue into his mouth. He gripped the back of her head, holding her close, kissing her deep and hard.

She straddled his thigh pressing her wet panties against him, showing him she was just as turned on as he was.

He pulled away and glared at the clock, wishing he could freeze this moment.

"There's not enough time." Haley whispered against his neck, while her hand continued to stroke him.

"That feels good, baby."

Forking his fingers in her silky blond tresses, he pulled her back in for another kiss. Nothing had ever felt this good, this right to him. He'd been with hundreds of girls over the years, and not one had touched him and driven him out of his mind like she was doing right now.

He bent his leg, and he felt her body quiver. She ground her pussy against his thigh. She was wet, her sweet essence soaking the thin cotton booty shorts she had worn to bed.

"Like that?" He whispered against her lips and he tried to focus on her pleasure while holding back his own that was threatening to wash over him any minute.

"Yes. That feels good." She breathed out the word and the sound went straight to his dick. She went wild, rubbing against him like an animal, lost in the sensation of her impending pleasure.

"Jayden!" She cried out and gripped his cock in a death clench as she came against his leg. It sent him over the edge with her.

Jayden thrust his cock in her hand, growling as he came hard.

She melted against his chest, her hand still on his cock. He nuzzled his nose against her soft golden hair, soaking in her scent, wanting to remember this perfect moment with her.

She looked up at him with bedroom eyes and gave him a satisfied smile.

"That's a nice way to start the day." She raised up and kissed him

Jayden swiped her hair away from her eyes and smiled, his heart tugging in his chest. "Yes. I can say I've never ever started the day off like that."

"Really?" She arched her brow, looking as if she didn't believe him.

"Yes." He nodded.

Her face broke into a beautiful smile. "Me either."

"Good." Jayden kissed her, thirsty for another taste of her.

Haley pulled away and sighed. "I need to get in the shower."

Jayden let her slide out of the bed, watching as she sauntered out of the room. He glanced under the sheet and shook his head. He was already hard again.

Haley breezed through the day with a lingering smile on her lips.

Funny how an orgasm could do that to a girl. Even Dana commented on her appearance, asking if she had changed her hair or gotten a facial.

It wasn't just the orgasm that had her smiling all day—it was Jayden. If he could make her body do that with her clothes on, she wondered how much more intense it would be with her clothes off.

She exited her last class of the day and her gaze immediately landed on Jayden.

Their eyes met. It didn't go unnoticed that he let his gaze travel the length of her body in male appreciation. Her heart thudded loudly in her chest at the unveiled lust in his eyes.

He closed the distance between them, striding purposefully toward her. He stole her breath as he closed his mouth over hers in another scorching kiss that she felt all the way to her toes.

He pulled back and smiled. "Since it's Friday night I made reservations at this fancy restaurant downtown."

Her eyes widened. "You did?"

"I did. How long will it take you to get ready?"

"Can you give me an hour?"

"Sure. But we need to make sure you don't get distracted or we'll lose our reservations." He chuckled. "They were very hard to come by."

"You're the one that needs to make sure you don't get distracted, not me." She teased as they walked along the sidewalk. The brilliant spring day carried the sting of a cool breeze, but she didn't feel a thing. Her body was warmed by Jayden's nearness.

"You're probably right. It's not safe for us to spend too much alone time together." Jayden laughed and tucked her hand inside his much larger one, coaxing her into a walk.

"Why should you be scared of little old me?" She gave him an innocent look.

"Said the spider to the fly." He cut his eyes at her.

She let a laugh slip out. It was freeing to be so relaxed and feel safe in public. "So since you won't let me have my way with you, you're going to at least wear your new clothes we picked out for you."

He didn't hide his grimace.

"Deal's a deal."

"Okay, but don't put that pink shirt on me."

She grinned. "It's not pink, it's coral."

IT REQUIRED some concentrated effort for Jayden to keep his eyes on the road instead of stealing glances at Haley as they drove to the restaurant.

He hadn't stopped looking at her since she walked into the living room wearing a fitted black and blue dress that stopped just above her knees. She wore black heels that accentuated those long legs of hers.

Her blonde hair fell in waves like silk across her shoulders and she was wearing that damn cherry lip gloss that drove him crazy. She'd put on more makeup than she normally wore. She looked like a model straight from the pages of a magazine.

"Go ahead admit it." Haley looked at him and grinned.

"Admit what?" He jerked his gaze back to the road. Had she caught him staring?

"That you like your new clothes." She waved her hand at him as the smirk lingered on her pretty lips.

"You were right." He smoothed his hand down the button-up shirt in the light brown pattern. It was not something he would have ever picked out for himself, but once he put it on, he liked it. "You really have an eye for putting clothes together. I can see why you chose fashion design as your major."

"Thanks." She glanced out the window. "I didn't realize Fayetteville had so much to do at night."

"College towns usually do." He glanced at her. "It's probably not much different from LSU."

A shadow of sadness passed across her eyes.

"Tell me something you and your friends did at LSU that you miss."

A smiled played at the corner of her lips and her eyes grew dreamy. "We used to go to this one bar in town on Thursday nights. It was just a hole in the wall, but we would play pool and dance." She looked at him. "I guess that's what I miss the most. The dancing."

Jayden swallowed. Dancing. The one thing he hated was the one thing she loved.

"Do you dance?" she asked.

"No."

"What do you mean 'no'?" Haley frowned.

"I mean I don't. I don't know how."

She laughed softly. "Everybody knows how to dance, Jayden."

He shook his head. "No, not everybody."

She stared at him for a minute before looking back out the window. The street was illuminated by streetlights, as people huddled together in groups near the bars and restaurants and shops. Jayden admitted that it looked quite cozy and quaint.

He hoped their restaurant turned out to be just as special.

Haley glanced around the swanky restaurant with candlelit linen-covered tables. Anthony had never taken her someplace like this. He always wanted to go to the sports bar during the football season and go fishing with his buddies in the summer.

"Have I told you how beautiful you look?"

Haley grinned and took a sip of wine. She had been

surprised when Jayden had ordered a bottle for them. She suspected he was more a beer guy.

"You told me at home. But it's always nice to hear it again." She thought she was going to go up in flames when she saw Jayden standing there in his button-up shirt and jeans. He'd even worn the dress shoes she'd picked out instead of those biker boots he always wore.

"You look stunning." His deep voice had her heart racing.

She held his gaze. "You look pretty hot yourself."

He gave her a sexy grin. "Must be the new clothes."

"I've seen you wear much less." She shook her head. "Trust me, it's not the clothes."

"Careful, my dear, don't taunt the wolf. He bites." He shot her a devilish grin across the table. "I'm not scared. I've survived worse." Jayden's smile faded.

The mood was gone.

He didn't like to be reminded of that night he'd rescued her. "Look, here we go." Jayden's voice had her looking up as their server set their plates before them.

"This looks really good." Haley cut off a sliver of her filet. She moaned as the flavor exploded on her tongue. "Oh, my God. That's really good."

Jayden grinned. "Go ahead, admit it."

"Admit what?"

"That I have really good ideas." Jayden took a bite of her steak and grinned.

Haley sighed. "Okay fine. This was a good idea." She took a sip of her wine. "All that means is you're going to have a hard time coming up with something that tops this."

"I can always top this, don't you worry. You haven't seen anything yet."

"You okay walking in those shoes? They look painful."

Jayden scowled at Haley's sky- high heels. He wasn't sure how she could take a step without breaking her ankle.

"Are you kidding? They're the most comfortable heels I have." Haley laughed.

The street was bustling with groups of college kids heading for the bars and couples dining at tables outside under the stars.

"Jayden!"

Jayden's head snapped up at the sound of his name. His gaze drifted to a couple dining at one of the outside tables. His lips spread into a slow smile as he met the gray eyes of the tattooed guy who was sitting next to a pretty blonde. The two definitely didn't seem to match.

Jayden guided Haley towards the couple.

"Braxton, what are you and Kate doing in Fayetteville?" Jayden kissed Kate's cheek and shook Braxton's hand as he gave him a shoulder hug.

"Kate has her annual bed and breakfast meetings with the other Arkansas owners. We've been here all week." Braxton's gaze slid over to Haley and his brows shot up in surprise.

"Oh, sorry; this is Haley Guthrie. Haley, these are some friends of mine, Braxton Devereaux and Kate Wolph"

"Nice to meet you, Haley." Kate skirted the café table and gave her a friendly hug. Jayden saw the surprise flicker in Haley's eyes at Kate's warm reception. At that moment his respect for Kate grew immensely.

"Hi, Haley." Braxton shook her hand gently.

"Nice to meet you both." Haley smiled at Kate. "Wow, you own a bed and breakfast. Where is it located?"

"Eureka Springs. It's called the Bella Luna." Kate beamed.

From the look of excitement on Kate's face, business seemed to be going well for her.

"I've never been to Eureka Springs, but I've heard it's lovely," Haley said. "And very romantic," Braxton added, giving Jayden a knowing look. "You two should check it out."

Jayden glared at his friend before looking at Kate. "Haley's not from Arkansas so I'm trying to show her around. She transferred here from LSU."

"Geaux Tigers." Braxton grinned broadly. He received a lot of dirty looks from people sitting around them.

"Easy, dude." Jayden laughed. "You better watch what you say around here. The Hogs rule here."

"That's what I've been trying to tell him." Kate arched her brow. "I told him he's in enemy territory. I thought he was going to get us kicked out of the B&B get-together last night. The talk soon turned to football and Braxton, being a diehard LSU fan, practically told everyone that the Hogs didn't have a chance this year."

"This is why we are not invited to dinner with them tonight." Braxton brightened.

Haley's mouth dropped open. "They really didn't invite you to dinner?"

"Yep."

"Thanks for the heads up. Guess I'll keep my favorite team to myself." Haley reached in her purse and pulled out her key ring with the LSU emblem and dangled it in front of him.

"Hell, yeah." Braxton gave her a fist pump before turning his attention back to Jayden.

"I heard you joined the Guardians," Braxton asked while the two women chatted between themselves. "You like it?"

"Yeah." It surprised him how much he liked his job. "It's steady work and it pays damn good." Though he hadn't really thought much about the pay. He didn't have any bills since he lived at the Guardian compound. The only major purchase he'd made was the Harley that was required for all the Guardians.

"You thinking about joining?" Jayden cocked his head and studied the Were. There was a peace about him since the last time he'd seen his friend.

Braxton had been accused of murder and had been on the run from the Louisiana Assassins, whose only job was to seek out and kill him. Braxton had been lucky enough to end up on Kate's doorstep after he'd been shot with a silver bullet. She had saved his life. It all ended with Braxton being declared innocent of all charges by Barrett, and the real murderer arrested.

Braxton shrugged. "Maybe. I know Barrett is looking for more Guardians in my area. I feel indebted to the guy for saving my ass."

"Barrett isn't the kind of guy who calls in his debts. He would be more concerned that you were committed to staying in the area and being loyal to the pack."

Braxton glanced at Kate, a softness floating into his expression. "I'm committed. That I know for sure. I'm not going anywhere."

Jayden saw the way Braxton gazed at Kate and his heart ached for something he knew he wasn't going to have, not now, not ever.

"So what's the deal with Haley?" Braxton elbowed him in the side while keeping his voice low. "She's not your usual type."

"And just what is my type?"

"I don't know. Loose, fast, those bikini model types that moon over you like you're the latest thing out of Hollywood."

Jayden opened his mouth, ready with some smart-ass comeback, but stopped. Braxton was right. Those were the types he usually attracted. Grabbing Braxton by the arm, he pulled him a few feet away from the girls and the crowd of people.

"I'm here protecting Haley." He kept his voice low. "Barrett sent me over here. Some asshole has been stalking her."

Braxton straightened, his expression hardened. "How long has this been going on?"

"Since she transferred from LSU." Jayden propped his hands on his hips. "You remember that second girl that was kidnapped after Ava?"

"Yeah." Braxton nodded.

"That was Haley."

"Fuck." Braxton ran his hand through his black hair with dyed blue tips. He met Jayden's gaze. "What can I do to help?"

Jayden shook his head. "Nothing right now. I had to move her from her dorm to the house where I'm staying. He's been leaving notes on her dorm door that have been getting more aggressive. Hell, he even managed to leave a note on my car while we were in the mall." Jayden told Braxton what the note said and about the DNA that was left on it.

"That's some fucked up shit." Braxton shook his head, anger etched in his face. The ex-bartender had a protective streak when it came to women. It stemmed from years of abuse his father had inflicted upon his mother.

"Look we are here for another few days. Let me know if you need backup."

"Thanks man. I appreciate the help."

"It's the least I can do after all you guys did for me when I was in trouble."

Jayden looked over at Haley, who laughed as she talked to Kate. "I'm going to find that asshole. And when I do, there's not going to be anything left of him when I'm finished.

"I feel ya, man. Hell, I'll even help you bury the pieces."

"What are you guys talking about? Jayden's new clothes?" Kate walked over and wrapped her arm around Braxton's waist. He pulled her close, keeping a possessive hand on her hip.

"Yeah, man. What's up with the new clothes?" Braxton arched his brow.

"That's my doing." Haley grimaced. "I told him he needed a fashion intervention."

"You did well. Jayden, you look like you stepped off the cover of *GQ* magazine." Kate nodded.

"Hey, there's nothing wrong with T-shirts." Braxton protested and glanced down at his own black T-shirt.

"I have nothing against T-shirts, as long as they're not the same shirt in different colors." Haley shrugged.

Braxton cut his eyes at Jayden and barked out a laugh. "She totally busted you."

"Leave Jayden alone." Kate elbowed Braxton in the side. "I might get Haley to give you a makeover. We still have that dinner tomorrow night with the Arkansas Historical Society. All you brought was black tees and jeans."

"Hey now, let's not get crazy." Braxton held up his hands, looking a little uncomfortable. Jayden snorted.

Haley cocked her head and studied Braxton. Braxton squirmed under her gaze.

"You could wear an unbuttoned vest over a black T-shirt and black jeans. Or you could wear a gray cardigan over your tee shirt. Either way, just make sure you wear dressy shoes."

Braxton lifted his brows, as if considering her suggestions.

"Wait a minute. You wouldn't let me wear any of my T-shirts." He jerked his thumb in Braxton's direction. "Why are you letting him get away with it?"

"You didn't have one black T-shirt. All you had were colored shirts from—"

"The mall." Braxton, Kate and Haley spoke in unison.

Jayden rolled his eyes. "Whatever."

Braxton laughed and slung an arm over Haley's shoulder. "I like you, Haley. Not only are you a fellow LSU fan, but you've got excellent taste."

Jayden growled and unwrapped the Were's arm from Haley. Braxton might be his friend, but that still didn't mean it was okay for him to touch her.

"What are you guys doing tomorrow besides the whole dinner thing?" Jayden looked from Kate to Braxton effectively changing the subject.

"No plans," Kate answered. "What did you have in mind?"

"We were thinking about checking out some of the local bars."

"We were?" Haley jerked her gaze up to him.

"Haley is quite the pool shark." Jayden winked at her.

"Pool and beer. Count us in." Braxton smiled.

"I've never played pool." Kate arched her brow.

"No worries. I'll teach you." Braxton gave her a wicked look. Jayden knew where their lesson was going to end up. In the bedroom with Braxton's stick.

"What time should we meet?" Jayden shook his head trying to dislodge the disturbing image from his head.

"Dinner is at seven. So let's say seven ten." Braxton deadpanned.

"Braxton, you're not getting out of dinner!" Kate elbowed him in the side.

"Fine. Eight thirty." Braxton rubbed his ribs.

"I'll text you guys when we get there." Jayden and Haley said their goodbyes before making their way down the sidewalk.

"So were you really planning on taking me to a bar or did you just come up with that when you saw your friends?" Haley cut her eyes at him.

"I had been thinking about it. I wasn't sure how safe I would feel with you and all those college guys around. But now I've got Braxton for backup, I think it'll be good." Jayden shrugged. "Your friends are very nice. I like Braxton's mate."

"Kate saved Braxton's life a few months ago when he got into a scrape."

Haley cut her eyes over at Jayden. "You're talking about the whole Assassins trying to kill him?"

Jayden stumbled to a halt. "How'd you know that?"

"I'm from Louisiana, remember. Plus my ex-boyfriend's father is pretty high in command. The pack is not very discreet when it comes to handling their business. Everyone heard about how the Assassins tried to kill Braxton in Arkansas territory. They said Barrett blew into Louisiana and threatened to kill the Pack Master if he ever thought about crossing into his territory without his permission again."

"Shit. I had no idea."

"Barrett really rattled the Pack Master, to the point that he started sleeping with guards around his bed." Haley grimaced. "I guess when I went to see Barrett after I started getting the letters I wasn't really sure how he was going to react."

"Did Barrett scare you?" Jayden scowled, fisting his hands at his side.

Haley shook her head. "The other Guardians tried to intimidate me when I tried to get into see him. There was one, Damon, who finally let me in." Haley laughed. "I guess they thought I was like Dana, trying to get in to sneak a peek at the Guardians working out."

Jayden took her hand and they continued their stroll along the sidewalk.

"Don't get me wrong, Barrett is scary. I mean there is something lethal about him. I know a lot of the females swoon over him, but they all keep their distance. But there is a justice and ethical code that he has that a lot of the other Pack Masters have forgotten." Haley shrugged. "He listened to me while my old Pack Master wouldn't have even given me the time of day.

I count myself lucky to be here in Arkansas."

Jayden nodded. She was right.

Barrett was a great leader and protector of the Arkansas pack. But there was something else Jayden's instincts told him. He never wanted to be on the receiving end of Barrett's dark side.

CHAPTER 8

*O*nce they arrived back at the house, Haley hurried to change into something more comfortable. When she walked in the living room, wearing her favorite red silk pajamas, Jayden froze.

"What's wrong?" She did a quick glimpse downward, making sure she hadn't missed a button. Nope all buttoned up.

"Nothing." He cleared his gravel throat. "You feel like watching a movie?"

"Sure. As long as it's not *The Waterboy*." She rolled her eyes.

Jayden frowned. "What's wrong with *The Waterboy*? It is a typical college movie, you know."

"Yes, but it's not funny after the fortieth time. That's all Anthony wanted to watch." She shook her head. "We always had to watch what he wanted to watch. I don't think I've seen a chick flick in over a year."

Jayden gave her wary look. "How do you feel about

Olympus Has Fallen?"

"I love that movie."

"But it's not a chick movie."

"But it has action and Gerald Butler. Those two things I can handle." She smirked.

"Gerald Butler, huh?" Jayden aimed the remote and the movie started playing. "I would have figured you for a Brad Pitt kind of girl."

"Definitely not." She reached for the popcorn bowl off the coffee table and set it between them on the couch. "Let me guess, you're a Megan Fox kind of guy."

"Nope, wrong." He smirked before munching on some popcorn.

"Really?"

"Yeah, I'm more into blondes." He gave her a long look.

So he liked blondes, did he? That was good. That was very, very good.

JAYDEN REACHED for the remote and turned off the TV. He glanced down at Haley asleep and snuggled against his chest. Her blonde hair fell over her eyes as her lips parted slightly.

Her hand was pillowed under her face and rested over his heart

He didn't want to move. He wanted to stay like that and watch her sleep until the sun came up.

She was breathtakingly beautiful. And she was so much more. She was strong. He'd known that from the first time he laid eyes on her, when her abductors had tied her to that filthy bed.

After what she had been through, Jayden saw a strength

inside her that made her want to keep going and not hide forever.

And when he was with her, he felt something he wasn't sure he had ever felt.

He felt whole, like she'd been the glue to mend what had broken inside his chest.

That singular thought rocked him to his naked soul. Haley wasn't for him. She deserved someone who wasn't fucked up like him.

He closed his eyes and laid his head back, staring up at the white textured ceiling. Even when they were getting each other off in bed, he had made sure to keep himself covered. He didn't want her to see his scars. He didn't want her to know.

He breathed out a heavy sigh, hugging her closer.

When the time came, he'd let her go. He had to. But for this moment, he just needed to hold her just a little while longer.

Haley blinked against the morning light streaming through the window. She glanced to the right, but Jayden wasn't there. She knew he wouldn't be. She used to have nightmares all night, dreaming about the one man that threatened to harm her.

When Jayden slept beside her, she slept soundly through the night. He had somehow kept the monsters at bay.

She flung back the covers and padded into the kitchen. Jayden, dressed in jeans and a black T-shirt, sat on a barstool with the cell phone pressed to his ear and his face fixed in a scowl.

Her heart hitched. Maybe it was Barrett with bad news.

"Granny, I'm sorry I didn't call. I've been busy with this new job." Jayden ran his hair through his hair.

Haley breathed out a sigh of relief and headed for the coffee pot. Jayden looked up and met her gaze.

Her heart melted as his lips quirked up.

"You know I can't tell you where I am." Jayden rolled his eyes and then sobered. "Please tell me you haven't been harassing Barrett about my location."

Whatever Granny said next had Jayden's scowl back in place. Haley bit her lip and wondered at the dynamic between the two. She knew that Granny was his only living relative and that when he'd moved to Arkansas, Granny moved with him. But that day at the party she sensed that things between them were strained.

She doctored her coffee with sugar and creamer before heading over to the bar stool and sitting.

"Fine. I'll tell her." Jayden hung up and gave Haley a look of disbelief.

"What's wrong? Is Granny okay?" She took a tiny sip of her coffee. The hot liquid warmed her as it slid down her throat.

"Granny told me to tell you that your order is in."

Haley felt her face blaze. She had forgotten all about that damn vibrator she had let Dana talk her into buying at Granny's sex party.

"What I can't figure out is how the hell she knew I was with you?"

Haley cleared her throat, thrilled he wasn't going to ask her exactly what she had ordered.

"Are you sure Barrett didn't tell her? Maybe she was

worried and Barrett wanted to put her mind at ease." Haley placed her coffee on the island counter.

"Maybe." Jayden's blue eyes narrowed on her. "Guess what else I didn't know?"

"What?"

"That you ordered something." He reached across the island and ran his finger across her wrist. She knew he could feel her pulse jumping under his finger.

Haley shivered and she pushed her coffee mug away. She was suddenly hot all over and no longer in the mood for coffee.

"I need to go get ready for class." The words came out as a whisper. Her heart pounded in her ears like a drum and warmth crawled around in her stomach.

"No, you don't. It's Saturday. You don't have class today." Jayden leaned over the island, dangerously close to her cheek.

She licked her dry lips.

His gaze dipped to her mouth. His nostrils flared.

She was in trouble. Deep, dangerous trouble.

"Haley, you didn't answer me."

Her eyes lifted to meet his gaze. "Maybe because you didn't ask me very nicely."

Jayden stood, his large muscled frame making the kitchen seem small. A predatory smile crossed his lips. "Is that right?"

"Yeah."

"I'm not a very nice guy." His muscles rippled under that damn skin-tight T-shirt as he took a step toward her.

She eased off the stool, keeping her eyes on him.

Haley took a step back, her heart beating in her ears. She could smell his scent, ocean and male. She'd memorized that scent the first night he'd come to rescue her.

"Haley." He advanced, but Haley took another step back.

"Are you afraid, little wolf?" His heavy-lidded gaze looked

her up and down. He didn't seem to care that he was being very obvious.

"I'm not afraid." Haley took another step away, but her back pressed hard into the hallway wall. She glanced away. She was trapped.

"You can't get away from me now."

"I wasn't trying to get away from you." Her chest heaved against the thin cotton of her pajamas. Lust flooded her veins. "Then what do you call it?" He leaned in, his breath tickling her cheek.

"I was teaching you to dance." Her face heated a thousand degrees. "You said you didn't dance. I was showing you. It's just two people moving their bodies together."

His gaze darkened. "I definitely like the sound of that." She was in over her head. Hell, the water was up to her eyebrows.

"Although, I know a better way than dancing to move our bodies together."

She went wet, her core throbbing at his promise of pleasure. She was going to explode if he didn't touch her.

He bent his head, nuzzling the crook of her neck. She moaned, her eyes drifting closed.

"Tell me what you bought," he whispered against the shell of her ear.

"Why?"

"Because my imagination is driving me crazy."

She pressed her palms against the wall to keep from touching him.

"Guess."

He laughed low and deep.

"Okay. Little wolf. I'll play your game." He brushed his lips across her bare shoulder where her top had slipped off. "Did you buy something sexy to wear?"

"No." Her heart raced as she leaned into him.

"Tell me. Don't make me get nasty with you. I just might make you blush."

"I doubt that." Haley squeezed her thighs together, stilling the growing ache.

"Did you buy a dirty movie?"

Haley felt her face heat as Jayden nipped at her collarbone. "Guess again."

He groaned against her throat sending tiny shivers throughout her body. Her head lolled to the side, giving him full access.

"Tell me." He cupped her cheek forcing her to meet his gaze. Looking into those aqua blue eyes was like truth serum.

"I bought a vibrator."

His nostrils flared as a low growl rolled out.

His face was strained with lust and looked as if he were holding onto his last thread of restraint. She didn't want him restrained. She wanted to see Jayden wild and out of control.

She leaned forward and brushed her lips across his whiskered cheek. "I bought a vibrator to get myself off. I was tired of people telling me no one else was going to touch me. So I decided to do it myself."

His lips, hot and soft, crashed down across hers. His tongue sought out hers in a dangerous dance as he pulled her tight against his hard body.

She moaned and ran her hands up his chest and laced her fingers around his neck. Her nipples hardened as she arched against him. His fingers found the edge of her top and slid under, to stroke her back.

"Take your shirt off." Jayden licked her neck. She arched against him, dizzy with lust.

"You do it. I don't want to stop touching you." Her fingers ran under his T-shirt and played with the deep muscled grooves of his abs.

He pulled away and gazed down at her. His fingers found the top button of her shirt and skillfully slid the button free. She watched his large hands, marveling at how good he was going to make her feel with those hands of his. When the last button was free, Jayden looked at her, his hands gripping her waist.

"Let me see you Haley. Let me see those pretty nipples that have been driving me crazy since I saw you."

Feeling more desirable than she had in a very long time, she slid her top off her shoulders, baring herself before Jayden.

Jayden moaned, his intense gaze glued to her breasts. His hands tightened on her waist. He was asking her permission to touch her. He was giving her control.

"Touch me," Haley breathed out.

"Tell me how you want me to touch you." She swallowed, her throat dry from gasping with desire every time he touched her.

"I want you to touch my nipples with your hands and then your mouth. That's how I want you to touch me."

Like a tornado rising out of nowhere, Jayden's blue eyes darkened. He released her waist and she almost slipped down the wall in a puddle.

Her gaze dipped from his eyes as his hands reached out. His fingertips brushed her nipples so softly she thought she would orgasm from a simple caress.

"So fucking pretty." His voice, rough and ragged, fueled her out-of-control desire for him.

His fingers traced her nipple in tiny torturous circles until she ached. He moved his attention to the other nipple, teasing the hard bud and making her writhe under him.

"Jayden, please." She grabbed his wrists and pressed her breasts into his palm.

"What do you need, baby?" Jayden whispered, his gaze locked on hers.

"I need more. Touch me more." She arched her pelvis into his and he growled.

"You have very sensitive nipples. Does that feel good?"

"Yes," she hissed. "That feels so good." She reached between them and grabbed his cock through his jeans.

"Easy, baby. You're going to make me come too soon if you keep touching me like that."

"More. I want more."

He cupped her breasts in his hands, his fingers tweaking her nipples. A moan escaped her lips at the delicious sensation he was creating. Lust tingled between her legs until she thought she was going to combust.

He bent his head and sucked her nipples between his soft lips. She cried out, the pleasure was so intense. She tightened her grip on his cock through his jeans. A low groan slipped past his lips.

She pulled his head against her breast. He licked and sucked and then moved to the next nipple.

"I need more, Jayden." Her fingers slid down to his jeans and unzipped him. She felt the head of his cock brush the back of her hand. She wrapped her hand around his thick shaft and she felt him tremble underneath her fingertips.

"Fuck, baby, you are going to kill me."

She tried to drop to her knees, but he grabbed her arms, his eyes wild.

"I want to taste you."

"Haley, I…"

"Do you not want me to put my mouth on you?" She held her breath, her fear of rejection once again seeping into her heart.

Jayden pressed his forehead to hers as his breath brushed

across her skin. "I want nothing more than to feel that hot mouth on me, Haley. But I'm... flawed."

She frowned as she looked up into his eyes. At once she saw fear and indecision.

"Everyone is flawed, Jayden."

He shook his head. "No, not like me. I'm scarred."

It hit her. He wasn't rejecting her. He was afraid of being rejected.

"Blindfold me."

His head snapped up. "What?"

"If you don't want me to see you, then blindfold me." She squeezed his cock harder refusing to let him go. He twitched in her hand.

Indecision flickered in his gaze and she knew if he thought too long he wouldn't go through with it. She leaned in and licked his neck.

"Are you sure?" He pulled her away, searching her face for any hesitation.

"Yes."

He swung her up in his arms and strode into the bedroom. His bedroom.

Haley's stomach tightened with pleasure as he set her gently down on the massive bed. He eased onto the bed holding her face between his calloused palms and gazing at her like she was a precious treasure.

No one had ever looked at her like that.

She blinked back the emotions spilling into her chest. How long had it been since someone had shown her that she mattered, that she was valued, that she was worthy? "Beautiful." Jayden covered her lips with his in a blistering kiss. She dug her fingertips into his silky blonde hair, clinging to him with a neediness she'd never known.

When he pulled his mouth away, he reached for his scarf

on the nightstand. She'd talked him into buying that scarf when they'd gone shopping together.

He carefully folded the scarf and held it up to her eyes. He hesitated.

"I trust you, Jayden." She wrapped her fingers around his wrist and pulled him closer. He tied the scarf behind her head, surrounding her in total blackness.

His fingers slid from her head to her cheek, stroking and caressing. With her loss of sight, her other senses were heightened. His scent became more distinct as did the sensation of his hand stroking her skin.

"You are so beautiful." He covered her mouth with his, plunging his tongue inside hers leaving her breathless and hot and wet.

He pulled away and ran his thumb across her bottom lip.

The bed shifted and she realized he had stood. Reaching out, her hands found his unzipped jeans, his erection straining out. She pulled his jeans past his hips and she heard him step out and kick the pants away. The coarse hair on his thighs tickled her fingertips as she ran her hands up to his waist.

"Sit down on the bed." She commanded. He obeyed and she slid off the bed to kneel between his legs. The hardwood floor bit into her knees, but she soon forgot her uncomfortable position.

"You're so fucking beautiful." His fingers threaded in her hair guiding her mouth to his cock.

She moaned, the scent of his arousal making her wet.

Her hand found his thick cock and she gripped him tightly. Tentatively, she stuck her tongue out and swiped it across the head, his arousal exploding on her tongue.

Unexpectedly, she moaned and closed her lips around the tip sucking him deep into her mouth.

"That's so fucking sweet." Jayden's voice was husky and rough as he gripped her head, setting the rhythm for how deep he wanted her to take him.

Moving her mouth back, she licked underneath the broad head of his cock before dipping down to gently suck his balls.

"Does that feel good?" She wished she could see the expression on his face.

"Fuck yeah. That's really good."

She sucked him back in her mouth, while cradling his balls in her hand. Her fingertips brushed a raised patch of skin near his groin. Jayden stilled and she immediately knew it was the scar that he was so afraid of her seeing.

She popped him out of her mouth and pressed her lips to the injured flesh while keeping her free hand on his cock as she continued to stroke.

"Tell me what you like."

He thrust his hips against her hand and groaned.

"I want your mouth back on my cock."

She kissed a trail from his thigh back to his thick erection. She opened her mouth and sucked him deep. He pumped his hips against her mouth forcing her to take him deeper.

His balls were hot and tight under her fingertips and she knew he was close to coming.

So was she.

She never expected to be so turned on by giving a blowjob.

"Suck me deep like that." His fingers tightened painfully in her hair.

She moaned and sucked him harder, pulling on his cock with her mouth and hollowing out her cheeks.

JAYDEN EASED BACK on his elbows on the bed, his lungs heaving for oxygen as Haley devastated him with that wicked mouth.

He gritted his teeth, holding back his impending orgasm. He didn't want to come. Not yet. It felt too fucking good.

But she was relentless, torturing him with the erotic pleasure of her tongue, sucking and licking and swallowing.

"Haley, sweetheart. You're going to make me come." She hummed against his cock, intensifying his pleasure.

"Sweetheart, I can't hold back." His balls tightened painfully and he knew he only had a few seconds.

"Haley, move. Or I'm going to come in your mouth."

She didn't budge. That little vixen only sucked him harder and deeper into that hot mouth until he was so fucking dizzy.

Fuck yeah.

Heat swept from his balls up his body and he heard the roar of his heartbeat in his ears. His cock exploded, shooting his release into her mouth.

His head fell back against the mattress as his body started coming down from the high of the most intense blow job he'd ever had.

Haley crawled blindly up his body. Immediately Jayden grabbed her around her waist and tucked her underneath him. He tugged the scarf off her eyes.

A smile lingered on her lips and he couldn't help himself. He drove his tongue into her mouth, tasting himself on her hot tongue. He'd never done that before, but with Haley it was hot as hell.

"I didn't think guys kissed a girl after she went down on them?"

"I have never wanted to. Until you." Jayden moved his mouth to her neck, licking that rapid pulse point that was driving him crazy.

"So you liked that?" She hesitated.

"Liked it? I loved it. I almost blacked out when I came." Jayden took her mouth again.

"This. Needs. To. Go." Jayden pushed her pajamas down. She wiggled her feet loose and kicked the obtrusive bottoms to the corner.

He propped himself up on one elbow and looked down at her, his gaze running the length of her body as his hand trailed down between her breasts.

Her breath hitched in her throat.

He grinned, liking that sound a lot.

He moved his hand lower over her silky skin until he found the juncture of her thighs. He cupped her, feeling how ready she was for him.

"You're wet."

"Yes." She breathed out, arching her hips into his palm. "I want to take my time with you."

He pressed her back into the bed and inched his way down her slender body as his mouth explored every inch.

When he reached her thighs, he ran his hand across her pussy, feeling the heat through her pink panties.

The scent of her arousal went straight to his head like whiskey.

He pulled her panties down and then off, unveiling his present. This was way better than any fucking Christmas present he ever got.

He tossed her panties over his shoulder and positioned himself between her thighs. She was waxed, only a thin landing strip remaining.

"So pretty." He pressed a kiss above her sweet spot. She wiggled her hips, urging him to move his mouth further.

He grinned. She had tortured him with her mouth, now it was his turn.

"Jayden, please."

"How do you want me to touch you, baby? Hard, soft, fast, slow? How do you like it?"

"Do it all." She arched her hips up into his hand.

He slid down, pressing her thighs wide with his hands and looked at the beauty splayed before him. She was wet, her soft folds glistening under the dim glow of morning's dawn. She made his heart beat faster and his cock as hard as granite.

He pressed his lips to her inner thigh. Her scent set his blood on fire as he slid his tongue along her silky skin.

She moaned and tried to wiggle closer to his face. He grinned and pressed her down with his palm.

He kissed and nuzzled each thigh until she grabbed his hair.

He lost his control and went down on her.

He licked her one long stroke before flicking his tongue across her clit.

"Yes, Jayden. More," she moaned.

He licked and kissed her soft skin, her sweet wetness coating his tongue like candy. She tasted like his own personal angel. His own personal heaven.

His licks became faster as her whimpers grew louder. He licked and swirled the hardened bud. Haley bucked her hips, lost in her own personal ecstasy.

Her fingers fisted tighter in his hair and she ground against his mouth.

God, he loved her like this. Wild and demanding. And all his.

Mine. Jayden ground his erection into the mattress, trying to hold back his own pleasure.

"Please, Jayden."

He closed his lips around her clit and sucked.

Haley cried out, bucking against his mouth as she orgasmed, her flesh quivering under his hands and mouth.

He held her until she stopped shaking.

He crawled up her body and hovered above her. She pulled him down into a kiss.

"Thank you." Her lips curled up in a slow lazy grin.

"I should be thanking you." He brushed the hair out of her blue eyes with his fingertips. He loved how relaxed and happy she looked at that very moment.

She laughed softly and pressed his palm into her breast. He plucked the pretty pink nipple between his fingers. Her smile faded. Her pupils dilated with lust.

"We're not done." She reached between their bodies and grabbed his erect cock. "I see that you agree."

She pushed his mouth down to her breast. He happily complied, sucking her sweet nipple.

"God that feels good."

"You taste like sunshine." Jayden moved his mouth to her other nipple and nipped. Haley wiggled under him, nudging his cock to her sweet entrance.

"I need you, Jayden, inside me."

"Demanding little thing, aren't you?" He chuckled against her breast.

"I never knew it could be this good." She gazed up at him in wonder.

"Sounds like your experience was with the wrong male." Jayden growled at the thought of another guy between Haley's thighs.

He nudged his cock against her tight entrance and gritted his teeth. She was tight, really fucking tight.

"I don't have any experience." Jayden froze. Sweat popped out on his forehead. Surely he had misunderstood her. "What?" "You're the first guy I ever went down on. You're the first guy that's gone down on me. And you're the first guy that's going to be inside me."

He frowned as his scalp prickled.

"What do you mean?"

"Jayden, I'm a virgin."

CHAPTER 9

*D*amn. She should have just kept her big mouth shut.

"You're a what?" Jayden froze, his cock poised at her wet entrance, his hands gripping her slender hips while his gaze pierced her soul.

She wrapped her fingers around his wrists, afraid he was going to pull away. "Does it matter?"

"Hell, yes, it matters. If I had known you were a virgin I never would have made you do that." He closed his eyes.

"Do what? Suck your cock?" She arched her eyebrow and ground her pelvis against him.

His eyes popped open and he tried to pull away. She locked her legs around him, holding him to her.

"Haley, please." He ground out, his sharp blue gaze zeroed on her.

"Tell me you don't want me. Tell me you don't want to be inside me right now." She blinked back the tears, refusing to get her feelings hurt.

"It's not that simple."

"Yes, it is. Its two people that want to feel good, just for a moment. That's about as simple as it gets." She let her hands fall to the bed and grip the comforter. She bit her lip, watching his gaze trained on her hands. Hope swelled inside her. He still wanted her. Here was her chance.

She trailed her fingers to her stomach and up past her ribcage and cupped her breasts. She rubbed her nipple between her thumb and finger, sending tiny shocks of pleasure through her body.

Jayden swallowed, as his gaze locked on her. His breathing grew faster and she knew he was getting turned on by watching the play of her fingers.

"I want to feel you inside me, Jayden. Deep inside me." She wet her lips with her tongue and forced herself to hold his gaze.

"I've lost my mind when it comes to you." His voice was but a whisper. He covered her body with his as he once again found her mouth. Her nipples hardened as his chest rubbed against her.

He trailed kisses from her mouth to her cheek to her neck. "Why do you have to be so addictive?" he moaned against her skin. It sent shivers down her body. She dug her nails in his back.

"I want you inside me." He was so very close to being inside of her. Thank God they were werewolves and didn't need a condom. Werewolves didn't carry or transmit diseases of any kind. And the only time a female could get pregnant was when she went into heat.

"I'll try not to hurt you, baby." He caressed her cheek with his hand.

Haley reached down and brushed his hand out of her way and grabbed his cock. He hissed at her touch. She grinned and squeezed before rubbing his cock in her wet heat.

Jayden reared up holding the thick head of his cock in his hand and slowly guiding it between her thighs.

Haley moaned as he slowly entered, stretching her beyond anything she'd ever imagined. The sweet sting of pain and pleasure was almost too much to bear. She rotated her hips wanting more of him.

"So fucking tight," Jayden murmured reverently as a bead of sweat gathered at his temple. His biceps flexed as he tried to force his body from thrusting in deep.

"Don't stop." Haley arched her hips causing him to slip farther inside her body.

"Easy, baby." Jayden ground out the words through clenched teeth.

"I want all of you in me." Her body vibrated with impending pleasure. He was large. As he entered her he filled her untried walls with a burning pain, but she didn't want him to stop.

"Fuck. Haley. I don't know how long I can hold back. You feel so damn good." Jayden moved another fraction of an inch inside her.

She met his hardened gaze and wrapped her fingers around the back of his neck, pulling him down for a kiss.

He was torturing her, she needed him all of him. Haley hooked her ankles around the back of his thighs and pulled.

He thrust all the way in. She cried out. The burning pain soon gave way to building pleasure.

She dug her nails into his firm butt and wiggled against him.

"Baby, don't move." Jayden's hoarse voice was strained and he buried his face against her neck.

"I can't. It feels too good." She whimpered unable to stop thrusting her hips upward.

"It's going to be over too soon if you don't stop wiggling."

She bit her lip and closed her eyes, trying to will her body to stay still.

He pressed his forehead to hers, his breathing labored, his breath hot on her cheek. He pulled back and thrust slow, allowing her body time to stretch to accommodate his large size. It was blistering heat with each beautiful stroke.

He rose up, towering over her, his dangerous gaze dipped down to where their bodies were joined. He grasped her thighs spreading her wide.

"Look how beautiful your sweet pussy is, sucking my cock deep."

Haley moaned and followed his gaze, her body on fire from his touch. His massive length stroking slow and deep within her. It was erotic as hell.

"Touch your nipples for me, baby." Jayden lifted his gaze to her.

She was going to burn alive. She eased back on the bed and slid her hands to her breasts while keeping her eyes locked on Jayden. Lust licked through his eyes, scorching her with his passion.

She cupped her breasts. Jayden growled and thrust harder.

She was over any embarrassment. She got over that when she had her mouth on his dick.

She flicked her finger across her nipple, sending an electric shiver through her body. Jayden's eyes glistened, liking what she was doing.

She pulled her nipple between two fingers and moaned.

"Your pussy's so hot, it's like I'm buried in fire." He leaned over her, thrusting faster and deeper.

His mouth clamped down over a hard nipple and he sucked.

"Please don't stop." She clung to him, wrapping her legs

around his back. Every deep thrust sent shards of pleasure ricocheting through her system until she thought she was going to combust.

"That's it, baby. I want you to come for me. I want to feel you tighten around my cock." Jayden's heated gaze bored into her.

He thrust harder and faster, torturing her with pleasure.

"Jayden." Her body exploded into a million tiny sparkles of light as her orgasm coursed through her body, sending her on wave after wave of pleasure.

"Fuck." Jayden thrust hard as he violently came deep inside her.

She'd lost her virginity and she'd lost her heart in one heart-pounding moment.

JAYDEN LAY IN SILENCE, holding Haley in his arms as the scent of sex and light of dawn filled the room.

He'd never been more at peace.

Yet there were questions that needed to be answered.

"Why didn't you tell your family you were still a virgin?" With light fingertips, he caressed her soft creamy shoulder.

"When my parents and Anthony came to pick me up after I had been rescued, I thought they would act relieved that I was okay. But they didn't. They kept their distance. Even in the car ride home, my mom was crying and telling me how I had brought shame to our family by no longer being a virgin." Haley snorted. "She said no one from a decent family would dare marry me now."

"What?" Jayden tightened his grip on her, his anger rising swift and hard.

"When we got home, my boyfriend told me that he wished me the best, but that he could no longer date me. First my parents disowned me then my boyfriend."

"Fuck, Haley." He pressed a kiss to her head.

"Then when my parents had me transferred to University of Arkansas. I felt abandoned. I don't think I had a chance to get over my hurt and start living. And then the letters starting coming."

She glanced up at him, the pain and fear still lurking behind those beautiful blue eyes. "I did realize through all this that even if I had been raped I deserve to be with someone who would see me for me and not who my parents are or how much money they have."

His heart clenched in his chest. "You are worthy of love, Haley. You are to be treasured and protected and loved beyond your wildest fantasies." He gently kissed her lips.

He lay back and cradled her in his arms. Her fingertips drifted downward.

He smiled.

When her hand trailed over to his injured thigh, he froze, forgetting momentarily how to breathe.

"Jayden?" Haley lifted her head and looked at him. "How did you get your scar?" Her fingertips lightly touched the shiny uneven skin.

His gut clenched. Lost in their lovemaking he had forgotten that he was baring himself to her. He hadn't even thought to cover himself with a sheet.

He licked his dry lips.

"Please tell me." Her blue eyes penetrated his, imploring him to confide in her. There was no condemnation in her gaze, only trust and understanding.

"It happened the night I tried to rescue you."

She frowned and glanced down at his scar. He squeezed his eyes shut. He couldn't look at her. He knew the pattern of the scar; hell, he'd looked at it every night he'd gone to bed. The jagged edges started at his thigh and ran along toward the inside toward his balls. He should have counted himself lucky his cock and balls weren't burned up with scar tissue as well. The red wolves had shoved salt into the wound of his thigh, making healing impossible.

"After I killed that guy that tried to rape you, two other red Weres knocked me out. When I woke up, I realized I was in a different building. They proceeded to practice their golf swing

on my head while I was hung upside down."

"Oh, my God." Haley gasped.

There was no stopping the words now. Nope. Once he started he couldn't stop the flood of words coming out of his mouth. Maybe having the orgasm of his life had affected his brain.

"When that wasn't enough, they used their redneck version of shock therapy, hoping I would scream for mercy. They told me the second I screamed they were going to finish what they started with you." Jayden clenched his jaw, acutely aware that Haley had snuggled deeper into his embrace, her eyes watching him carefully.

"I told them to go fuck themselves. They decided to shock me instead." He chuckled mirthlessly. "The thing about shock therapy is that it locks up your muscles. Even if you wanted to scream you can't.

"All these months I felt like I had failed you because I couldn't rescue you. I thought they had raped you after they were done with me." Jayden brushed her hair behind her ear. A huge weight lifted off his shoulder, knowing she was safe.

Haley shook her head and looked away, clearly shaken by what he had just said. "After you killed that red werewolf, it wasn't fifteen minutes before a group of Guardians, Jaxon, Zane and Lucien burst through the door. I learned later they were from Arkansas. I asked them if they had gotten you out, but when they checked the building they couldn't find you."

Jayden nodded, his heart tugging. Even in her distress, she hadn't forgotten him.

"I had no idea they had done that to you, Jayden." She looked back at him. Her beautiful blue eyes were moist with unshed tears. "I'm so sorry. All of that is my fault."

"Baby, it's not your fault. It was those red wolves. And if I had to do everything over, I wouldn't do anything different. I'd take the pain if it meant you were safe."

A tear spilled down her cheek and he swiped it away.

She caressed his cheek with her hand. "So you really had no idea I was still a virgin? Yet you still wanted me?"

He narrowed his gaze. "Wanting you has nothing to do with if you are a virgin or not. I've been walking around with a hard-on since I saw you sitting in my Granny's house at her damn sex party."

"Really?"

"Yes. Damn, Haley, I don't think I've ever come that hard."

She leaned over him, bringing her mouth across his. She dipped her tongue into his mouth and kissed him thoroughly.

She reached between their bodies and grabbed his erection. "Feels like you're ready again."

"Baby, I was ready two minutes after I came." Jayden lifted her onto his lap, making her straddle him. She sat back on her heels and grinned down at him.

He lifted his hands, caressed her cheek and trailed his fingers down to her breasts. Her blonde hair hung in waves across her slim shoulders. Her blue eyes shone like a woman satisfied.

"You're fucking gorgeous, you know that?"

"So are you." She grinned and pressed her breasts into the palms of his hands.

He chuckled.

She eased down the foot of the bed.

"Where are you going?" He sat up on his elbow. He wasn't ready for her to go. And his cock certainly wasn't ready for her to go either, judging by how it was standing up at a ninety- degree angle.

"I'm showing you how gorgeous you are." She slid between his legs and spread his thighs.

"Wait…" His heart froze in his chest. It was the last place he wanted her.

She looked up at him, only inches from his cock. Keeping her eyes on his, she bent and kissed his uninjured thigh.

His cock twitched.

She moved right toward his scarred thigh. Jayden dug his hands in the sheets to keep from pushing her away. He didn't even like looking at the injury. He sure as hell didn't want her examining it.

She slowly turned her mouth and licked his balls with the tip of her tongue.

"What are you doing to me?" Jayden shuddered. "I'm going to kiss it and make it better." She turned her face, nuzzling her cheek against his scar before placing a gentle kiss on the rough skin.

His cock hardened to the point of pain, yet he forced himself to be still and watch her.

She kissed the twisted flesh. His heart clenched at the tender sight.

She ran her tongue along the length of his scar until she brushed against his balls.

"Damn, Haley."

"Does it feel better?" she whispered, her breath tickling his balls.

"Yes," he hissed out. Sweat popped out across his body as he strained not to touch her.

"Your scar isn't ugly. It's a sign of your strength. A sign of your courage."

"Right now my strength isn't that great. I'm not sure how much longer I can stay still with your mouth that close to me." Jayden swallowed.

"Be good and maybe I'll give you a treat."

Holy fuck. Was his little virgin talking dirty to him? He gazed down at her, her lips an inch from his dick, her breath caressing his balls.

He threaded his hand through her silky blonde hair and gently tugged. "Haley, come here."

She nuzzled his hand and turned her mouth towards his cock. Before she locked her lips around him she looked him straight in the eye.

"You come first."

"ARE you sure you still want to go out?" Jayden came up behind her, wrapping his arms around her waist.

"Yes, I'm sure." She turned in his arms and gave him an eye roll. "I had sex Jayden, not open heart surgery."

He frowned. "Yeah, but it's your first time and you may still be hurting."

"I'm not hurting. Just sore in all the right places." She waggled her eyebrows at him. Deep down her heart tugged at how considerate he was being.

"Did I hurt you?" He cupped her cheek. Her heartbeat picked up speed.

"No, you didn't hurt me. I should be asking you that. I might have bruised your penis."

He closed his eyes and sucked in a breath.

Haley bit back a smile. "Ah, so I see you can take a licking and keep on ticking."

"Stop talking like that." He groaned. "Or we'll never make it to meet up with Braxton and Kate."

Haley laughed. As much as she wanted Jayden naked, she

had also been looking forward to hanging out at the bar with his friends. Hell, she'd been looking forward to just getting out again.

The past few months she'd felt like she'd been living in a cave, too scared to leave her dorm room. She even worried about what she wore. One wrong move and she could piss off her stalker and get something worse than love letters.

She shook her head and glanced down at her designer jeans and fitted red top. She'd decided to wear her favorite red heels. When she'd walked into the living room earlier she could tell from the way Jayden was looking at her, that she'd made the right choice in her outfit.

"No way. We are not missing the opportunity for me to kick your ass in pool."

He arched a brow. "Kick my ass? I'd like to see that."

"Want to make a bet?" She grabbed her red purse and slung it over her shoulder.

"What did you have in mind?"

She crossed her arms. "If I win, you take me dancing. " She stuck her finger in the air. "And you actually have to dance.

You can't pay someone else to do it."

"Fine. But if I win, you have to go skinny dipping with me."
She smiled. "Fine."

"In the university fountain."

"What?" Haley's mouth hit the hardwood.

He smirked. "Unless you lose."

Haley shut her mouth and spoke through her gritted teeth.

"Fine."

Jayden's smirk slid off his face.

"What? You didn't think I'd agree?" She shrugged. "It's not like I'm going to have to do it anyway. I plan on winning."

Jayden's sexy smirk was back and it gave her stomach a tumble. Maybe they could meet his friends another night?

"Come on." Jayden took her hand and walked her out the door. "Braxton's already called to say they're getting there early. Seems like the bed and breakfast meeting didn't go so well."

JAYDEN WALKED into the crowded college bar with Haley at his side. He watched her face light up as she looked around at the people dancing to the band and playing pool. As much as he wanted to stay home and strip her naked, he was glad they came. She needed this.

He spotted Braxton and Kate in a corner booth. Braxton was nursing a beer and Kate a glass of white wine. As they made their way over to them, Jayden didn't miss the looks the college guys were giving Haley. He slid his hand from her waist to her hip and shot a glare at any asshole looking too long.

He couldn't really expect any male to keep his eyes off Haley; with her tight jeans and red shirt she was smoking hot. Not to mention her fuck-me red heels.

He definitely had plans for those heels when they got home. Braxton nodded when he saw them approach.

"How did you two beat us here?" Jayden let Haley slide into the booth first before settling in beside her.

Braxton gave him a pained look.

"It was going well until one of the men started talking about LSU and how they were going to suck this year." Kate sighed. "You would have thought they were talking about sacrificing Braxton's first born by the way he jumped up from the chair and started in on the guy."

"It's football. It's serious." Jayden snorted. "You can't trash talk about someone's team. It's like fucking their mate."

Braxton nodded and looked at Kate. "See. I told you."

Haley let out a laugh out. "I feel your pain, Braxton. But we are in Hog territory now. And when in Rome…"

"I know, I know." Braxton stood. "Come on, let's get the ladies some drinks. I got a feeling I'm going to need it to numb the pain of being around all these Razorbacks."

Haley watched Jayden and Braxton make their way to the bar. Every female within a twenty-foot radius turned, eyeing both males. Haley narrowed her eyes. "It gets easier once you're mated."

"I don't know what you mean." Haley jerked her head towards the pretty blonde.

Kate slid her gaze toward the two males. "You won't feel so jealous about girls looking at your man once you're mated."

Haley knew the rules. Once a male werewolf mated his chosen female he could never cheat on her. They would be forever faithful until death.

"I don't think we are headed in that direction. We're just having fun right now." Haley shook her head and smiled.

Kate fought a smile.

"No, really. It's not serious."

"Honey, anyone in this room that saw you two walk in knows it's serious." Kate cocked her head.

"What do you mean?" Haley's breath caught in her throat. Was it obvious that she'd fallen for Jayden?

"I mean I see how he can't keep his hands off you."

"It's Jayden. I may not have grown up here but his reputation certainly has preceded him. I know he's quite popular with the ladies." She forced a smile and swallowed back the bitter taste those words left.

"Really?" Kate wrinkled her nose. "Because when I met him in January, he was doing his best to get away from a group of oversexed ladies that were staying at my bed and breakfast."

Haley gave Kate her full attention. "For real?"

CHAPTER 10

Kate nodded and finished off her wine. "It was a group of writers. Romance writers. They stayed drunk and were continually trying to molest Jayden. Scared the poor guy to death."

"What about Braxton?"

"Oh, they tried with him too, but I made it very clear who he belonged to."

"So you've been mated for a while."

Kate waved her hand in the air in a dismissive gesture. "Oh no. We were not mated then. But I knew he was mine." She leveled her gaze at Haley. "When you know, you know."

"Okay, ladies. Chardonnay for Kate and Pinot Noir for the lady in red." Jayden winked as he set the glasses down on the table.

"Yeah, man. What's the damn deal letting her out wearing red?" Braxton elbowed him in the ribs.

Haley glanced down at her top. "What do you mean?" Jayden slid in beside her and rested his hand on her knees. "He means that red is the color all males seek out."

"You mean for male Weres." Haley took a sip. There were very few Weres that she knew of at the university.

"Honey, you don't have to be a Were to seek out the hot chick wearing red. All guys, Weres and humans alike, love red. It reminds them of sex." Braxton frowned "You know like those baboons with the big red asses. It means they want to mate."

Kate gave him an incredible look.

"What? I saw it on *Nat Geo*." Braxton shrugged.

Jayden took a drink of his beer. "He's right. I saw that same show. It has some fascinating facts on there."

Braxton nodded. "Did you know that more people are killed by donkeys every year than in an airplane crash?"

"A donkey is a mean son of a bitch," Jayden offered.

Braxton took another sip of his beer. "Goddamn right they are. I hate a fucking donkey."

Haley pushed her plate away and sighed. "I think I ate way too much."

"What do you mean? There's still half a burger left." Jayden pushed the plate back in front of her.

"No. I can't eat another thing." Haley shoved her plate at him. "Here you eat it. You're going to need your strength for when you lose the bet and you're going to have to go dancing." Jayden cringed.

"Dancing?" Braxton perked up sensing Jayden's discomfort.

"I didn't know Jayden liked to dance."

"He doesn't. But we made a bet. If I win, he has to take me dancing." Haley smirked.

"And if Jayden wins?"

Jayden watched Haley's smirk fade.

"I think I need to use the ladies room." Haley smiled.

"I'll go with you." Kate grabbed her purse.

The two men watched their ladies walk across the room to the bathroom.

"You don't dance, Jayden."

"No shit." He glared at Braxton.

"Which means only one thing." Braxton rubbed his chin.

"What's that?"

"It means that whatever you got her to agree to is a pretty good pay out for you."

"It is." Jayden felt a smile cross his face.

"Then you need to make sure you win, brother."

CHAPTER 11

"Come on, Jayden. I don't want you to let me win." Haley crossed her arms over her chest and watched as he missed his shot. "I want to win fair and square."

Jayden looked up and scowled. He wished he could tell her he was letting her win. But he had apparently underestimated Haley's talent on the pool table. Much like he'd underestimated her talent in the bedroom.

She was slightly ahead and winning.

Jayden rubbed the back of his neck, watching as Haley walked to the end of the table and leaned over to set up the shot. His gaze drifted down to her firm ass and he growled under his breath.

Braxton sidled up to him. "Get your head in the game, man, and off your woman's ass. Or else you're going to be ballroom dancing in a tux."

Jayden jerked his head over his irritating friend. "Ballroom dancing? Haley said nothing about ballroom dancing."

"Or salsa dancing. They're pretty popular right now with the chicks." Braxton took a long drink of his beer.

"You know you're really starting to frighten me with all your female knowledge on what's hot in the dancing world." Jayden snorted.

"Fuck off. We have a bed and breakfast. It's hard not to hear half the conversations females are having with their men about new things to try. Dancing always makes the top ten." Braxton shot him a glare.

"If they are looking for new adventures, maybe you should suggest having sex on a washing machine to liven things up." Jayden grinned. While he had stayed at the Bella Luna, Braxton and Kate had locked the laundry door while getting down to business. Granny would have walked in on them in the act if the door hadn't been locked.

"Maybe I'll add it to the list of things to do at the Bella Luna for the guests," Braxton deadpanned.

"I think it's your turn." Haley turned and caught his gaze on her ass. She arched her brow.

Braxton slapped him hard on the back. "Come on, man. Make this shot and you're back in the game. Otherwise you'll be putting on your dancing shoes, Fred Astaire."

Jayden shoved his beer at Braxton and picked up his stick. His gaze locked on the table as he analyzed which shot would put him in the lead.

He leaned over and took his shot, effectively sinking three balls.

"Yeah!" Braxton yelled.

Haley arched her brow and nodded. "Nice shot."

"Thanks."

Haley focused her attention back on the pool table her brow furrowed as she concentrated on her strategy.

She took her shot. She missed.

Jayden frowned.

"Your turn." She glanced up at him.

His gut tugged. Winning didn't seem so important anymore.

He trudged over to the other side of the table. He knew the next shot was an easy one. He slowly took his aim. His gaze drifted over the cue ball up to Haley. She balanced one foot on the rung of a high chair at the tiny round table where Kate sat.

Three college guys came over and stood in front of her, blocking Jayden's view.

He straightened and frowned.

The guys apparently said something that had Haley shaking her head and trying to walk around the group. One guy grabbed her arm.

All Jayden could see was red, his anger pouring through his body like a storm. He leapt and cleared the pool table and landed next to Haley. He shoved the guy, pushing him back a few feet.

"Don't touch her." Jayden growled.

The college dude bowed up. "It's a free country and she ain't wearing a ring. So that means she's free."

Rage filtered through every cell of his body. For a brief second he considered shifting into wolf form and ripping the prick's throat out. As much as he wanted to kill the human, he knew he couldn't shift. So he did the next best thing.

Jayden plowed his fist into the guy's face. The guy stumbled backwards and shook his head. He delivered a blow to Jayden's stomach. Jayden didn't feel any pain but remembered to double over so the humans wouldn't suspect anything. The other two college guys grabbed each of Jayden's arms, holding him while the guy punched him in the face.

Jayden looked up and grinned as blood dripped down his mouth. Anger and rage melded into his veins as he ached to break some bones. "Quit fucking around and hit me, you pussy."

The guy sputtered, looking stunned.

Braxton pulled one guy off Jayden and began to punch him until he was down on the floor. The other guy immediately let go of his arm and held his hands up as he backed away.

Jayden faced the guy who had dared put his hands on Haley and growled.

Everything happened so fast.

One minute some college guys were trying to hit on her and Kate, and the next thing she knew Jayden was leaping over the pool table and slugging one of them in face. She didn't even have time to scream.

Kate pulled her back as Braxton jumped in the fray, pulling one guy off Jayden and proceeding to pound the guy into the ground, his tattooed arms flying.

A crowd was quickly gathering and she knew it wouldn't be long before the cops arrived.

"They're going to kill them." Haley finally found her voice and tried to stop Jayden.

"Wait, don't get in the middle of it." Kate grabbed her arm.

"I'm not letting Jayden go to jail for me." Haley shot the woman a glare and snatched her arm free.

Haley ran to Jayden and threw her arms around his waist. "Jayden, stop!"

His muscles bunched and tensed under her palms as he viciously hit the guy in the face. His nose was obviously broken and both eyes were already bruising. She had to stop Jayden before he killed the guy.

"Jayden, please." She jumped on his back and wrapped her arms around his neck, hoping to get through his haze of fury.

She'd never seen him so mad, so out of control.

Haley pressed her mouth to his neck and bit down.

Jayden froze his fist in midair and let go of the guy's shirt.

The bloodied college guy slumped to the floor in a heap.

Haley slid off his back as the crowd grew silent.

Jayden turned and faced her.

She gasped. She couldn't help it. His lip was split and his cheek was starting to turn blue. But that's not what scared her.

It was his eyes.

They were turning colors, shifting to a yellow hue, icy with rage and anger and lethal intent.

Blood lust.

She stepped closer, his ragged breath brushing her face. She met his gaze.

"Are you okay?" She reached up and touched his bruised cheek with her fingertips.

He growled, and his angry mouth crashed down on hers as he thrust his tongue inside her mouth, claiming her.

She moaned, fisting her hands in his shirt, tasting his blood from his lip. She didn't pull away, she didn't want to.

"I hear the sirens, guys. We need to be leaving." Braxton nudged Jayden's shoulder. "You guys can make out at home."

He pulled away, his gaze on hers steady and unflinching as if he were silently communicating.

"Let's go." He tugged her hand, but she dug her heels in.

"What?"

"My purse." She pulled out of his grip and swiped her purse off the table and swung it over her shoulder before taking his hand.

He hurried out of the bar, the crowd parting for them. Haley didn't miss the appreciative way all the college girls were eyeing both Jayden and Braxton with a mixture of fear and want.

They stepped out onto the sidewalk. The crisp spring air leapt into their lungs. The tension between them seemed to ease a little.

Haley just hoped this wouldn't ruin the rest of their night.

JAYDEN COULD ALREADY FEEL his split lip mending itself. That was one good thing about being a werewolf; he had a quick recovery time.

He cast a quick glance at Haley as she fought to keep up with him in those strappy high heels.

He immediately slowed his gait. They were a few blocks away from the bar and getting caught now was probably not an issue.

Jayden wasn't sure what to say to her. He'd seen the look of fear in her eyes at what he'd done, at how out of control he had gotten.

He wasn't going to apologize for beating the shit out of that asshole. He'd put his hands on Haley. His brain had gone automatically alpha, his only wish to tear that guy's throat out.

But tearing out a guy's throat in front of a room of human witnesses would probably piss off Barrett. So Jayden had settled for a bare knuckle brawl.

"Hold up, Jayden. Kate wants to stop in here," Braxton called out.

Jayden stopped but didn't turn around.

"We'll be right back." From the corner of his eye Jayden watched Braxton and Kate enter the tiny ice cream shop. He checked his Luminox watch. It was almost midnight and the damn store was still open.

He shook his head and forced himself to look at Haley.

"They probably just said that to give us some privacy." He looked away.

"You scared me back there."

"I didn't mean to." He flinched. "But when I saw him putting his hands on you I lost it."

"That's not why I was scared."

He frowned and looked at her.

"I was scared you were going to get arrested, that they were going to take you away." The tiny hitch in her throat had him pulling her into his arms.

He kissed the top of her head She snuggled closer to his chest.

"Don't worry. I'm not leaving. You're still safe. And I promise I'm going to do everything I can to catch this stalker and then you're going to get your life back, baby. You're going to get your freedom back."

She pulled back and met his eyes, some unknown emotion crossing her features.

She nodded, lifted up on her tiptoes and pressed her lips to his.

He knew it was an innocent kiss, a gentle comforting kiss. But the second she touched him, all Jayden could think was, he wanted more.

Her lips parted and he slid his tongue against hers, kissing her with a bruising need.

Yet it wasn't enough.

Gripping her hips, he pressed into her, rubbing his cock against her willing body. She moaned and tugged him closer.

He was going to explode in his jeans. Right there in public.

She dug her nails into his scalp as their kiss turned frenzied. He growled, as his body demanded he take her.

"All right, all right. Am I going to have to separate you two?"

Jayden pulled back and glared. Braxton watched them with amusement as he licked a chocolate ice cream cone. Kate giggled as he held out the cone for her to taste and then snatched it away at the last minute to settle an open mouth kiss on her.

"You're the pot calling the kettle black." Jayden arched his brow and pulled Haley against him. "You really did get ice cream."

"Yeah. What'd you think I was making it up?"

Jayden shook his head and glanced at Haley, who was eyeing the ice cream cone. His erection strained against his zipper as he imagined her mouth on him

He took her hand as they walked down the sidewalk.

CHAPTER 12

"Where are we going?"

"To get ice cream."

"I'm sorry we didn't get to finish our pool game." Jayden pulled her into his embrace just as they entered the living room. She looked up loving the feel of his warmth against her. "You're just saying that because I was winning."

He laughed and shook his head. "Oh no, baby, I was ahead with my last shot, remember?"

Haley frowned. "Yeah, but before that I was ahead in the game. So, technically, I was winning. You just got lucky."

"There are no technicalities in pool. You either win or lose. And I won."

She pulled away and propped her hands on her hips. "I want a do over."

His face lit with amusement and surprise. "A do over?"

She nodded. "Yes, a do over. We play another game to see who the real winner is."

"You just want to get out of making good on your end of the deal."

She shifted her weight from foot to foot as her face heated. "No, that's not it."

"I think it is. I think you don't want to pay up. I won. I sunk the last ball before I leapt over the pool table."

"I never saw that." Her mouth dropped open.

"I did."

"Maybe I don't believe you." She narrowed her eyes.

His face broke into a wide smile and he pulled out his cell phone. "Okay, here, call Braxton. He'll tell you who won." She was sunk. She knew it.

Jayden had won their bet.

Which meant she was going for a late night dip in the campus fountain.

"Fine. Do you want to head on over to the fountain now? Or do you prefer to wait until class is in session?" She forced a smile.

Jayden laughed, the deep sound reverberating in the room.

She had never heard a sexier laugh.

"No. Not now. I'll let you know when I want to collect on my debt." His expression grew serious and he took a step towards her. "Although I think there is something else we can do to pass the time.

Her panties dampened at his unspoken promise of pleasure. The unmistakable look of lust in his eyes sent her heart into a frenzied rhythm as her body heated under his gaze. Her gaze dropped lower. The bulge against his zipper almost made her moan.

"What did you have in mind? Go Fish?" She licked her lips.

"Guess again." His gaze roamed down her body. She was glad she'd worn the fitted shirt that showed off her curves.

"I don't know. A board game maybe."

He shook his head in a slow decided motion. "Something with less clothes."

"Strip poker?"

"That does have an appeal, but I'm not sure I could concentrate on my hand." His gaze met hers.

She reached out and ran her palm underneath his button-up shirt. Her fingers skated across hard muscle and smooth skin. He growled.

"Then maybe you can concentrate on my hand." Her fingernail trailed up his chest and scraped his nipple. She felt the unmistakable tremble coarse through his body like a small earthquake.

He grabbed her hand, pressing her palm over his heart. His heartbeat was thunderous and she could feel it beat in his chest.

"You shouldn't tease me like that." His other hand slid down her waist and cupped her hip, nudging her closer.

Her body heated as need pooled between her legs. She wanted him, really, really bad.

His mouth slammed down across hers in heated passion that left her in a pool of need. She clutched his waist, holding for fear she'd be swept under the tidal wave of desire.

He groaned against her mouth and she ground her pelvis against his rock hard erection. His hands came down her back and palmed her ass and he lifted her into the air.

She wrapped her legs around his waist.

"I can feel how hot you are against my skin." He murmured against her neck and nipped the delicate skin.

"Do that again. Bite me again." With every scrape of his teeth across her skin it upped her pleasure tenfold.

"You like that, baby?" He nipped her flesh again.

"Yes." She tightened her legs around his waist, feeling every sinewy muscle against her thighs. "I need you inside me now."

He devoured her mouth with his kiss as he carried her into his bedroom. He laid her down on the bed and pressed his body along the length of hers. He rolled off, but she tried to drag him back.

"I need your clothes off." His voice was raspy as he lifted her top and tugged it over her head. Next came her jeans. She lay before him in only in her bra and underwear.

"Red." His pupils dilated.

She glanced down at her fire-engine red matching thong and bra. She had bought it months ago and never bothered wearing it. She didn't have a reason to. Not until now.

She gazed into his eyes, brimming with lust so violent she was afraid she wouldn't get enough.

Sucking up her courage, she ran her trembling hands up to her breasts and cupped them. His eyes followed the motion like an animal tracking its prey.

"Do you like that?" she whispered. Her heart beat in her ears like rushing ocean waves and she was pretty sure she was going to stop breathing from lack of oxygen in the room.

"Yes."

He sat mesmerized and unmoving.

"Jayden, take your clothes off."

He blinked and moved off the bed at her command. Keeping his gaze on her, he unbuttoned his shirt and slid it off his powerful broad shoulders. He moved to his jeans sliding them off his hips until he stood there before her naked.

He was magnificent. Big and broad like a linebacker yet sleek like a cover model. For this moment, he was all hers.

"Touch yourself." His sharp words bit into her internal daydream.

She blinked as her face heated at his command. He reached down and circled his straining erection and stroked.

Her breathing came in pants and she couldn't look away from his hand slowly moved along his shaft.

She slowly slid one hand down her stomach keeping her gaze locked on him. He growled as she reached the lace of her panties.

Dark pleasure shot through her as her finger brushed across her clit.

"Yeah. Like that. That's fucking hot." He growled low and deep.

Her breath hitched as her other hand circled her hardened nipple, teasing until she was burning with need. She pinched the hardened bud between her fingertips. A moan escaped her lips as pleasure zinged through her body.

A low groan of satisfaction erupted from Jayden's lips. His breathing had turned to a pant.

Fiery lust sparked from his blue eyes. He looked predatory and strong and gorgeous.

"Show me how you touch yourself when no one is looking, baby. When you are alone in your bed and you've pulled those sweet little panties off and you need to find some relief."

She swallowed. He was going to make her come with only his voice and vivid commands.

While her fingers plucked her erect nipple, her other hand slid under the waistband of her lace panties, her slickness coating her fingertips. She pressed her lips together, stifling a moan.

"Don't. I want to hear every little sound of pleasure you make." Jayden moved closer.

She circled her clit and stopped, afraid she was going to come too fast.

She pulled her fingers out of her panties and watched as Jayden stretched out on the bed, his face inches from her pussy.

She wanted to beg him to put his mouth on her and make her come. She knew he'd do it. But there was something else in his eyes, something darker

It made her wet pussy ache. She was going to give him what he wanted and in turn get what she deserved.

She reached up between her breasts and unsnapped her bra. She tugged the straps off her shoulder, tossed the garment to the floor and lay back down, keeping her eyes on his.

He moved between her legs and pressed his mouth to her inner thigh.

"No, not yet. You wanted to watch, Jayden." Sensuality radiated through her body.

She cupped her naked breasts and gently squeezed her nipples between her fingers.

"Show me what feels good, baby." Jayden watched with rapt attention while he stroked himself.

"It feels good when your mouth is on my nipples sucking hard." She plucked the buds between her fingertips.

"Hmmm. You like my mouth."

"Yes." She stared back at him. He began to crawl between her thighs, but she put her red high heel foot on his shoulder, stopping him. She hadn't realized he didn't take her shoes off.

"No. You're going to watch. And when I come you're going to put your mouth on me and make me come again."

His dilated pupils locked on hers and then drifted to her hands. He curled his hands into fists. His muscles strained and she knew he was having a hard time trying not to touch her.

She slid her fingertips behind her lace panties, the fabric skidding across her skin. She slid her fingers down between the wet silky folds and moaned.

"I want to see."

Haley pulled her fingers out and spread her thighs wide; acutely aware of how vulnerable she was with him. And how much more vulnerable she was about to get.

She tugged her lacy panties to the side. His jaw clenched.

"Touch yourself."

His voice, low and dark, sent shivers through her entire body. She reached down and trailed her fingers through her wetness. Another moan slid past her lips.

His gaze was locked onto to her fingers and his breathing grew rapid. He was like a predatory animal ready to seize his dinner.

She circled her swollen clit with two fingers and sucked in a ragged breath.

"That's so fucking hot." Jayden moved closer, spreading her thighs with his shoulders. He pressed a kiss to the side of her knees before turning his gaze back to her fingers.

"Is this what you do at night? When you're alone? Touch yourself?" His muscles strained in his bicep as he stroked faster.

It's what she did when she thought about him.

"Yes." She'd masturbated before but never had it felt this hot, this naughty.

"So pretty." He lifted her high heels across his shoulders, resting her knees by his head. His breath tickled her clit and she arched up to his mouth.

"Jayden, please." She struggled against his hand planted on her stomach pressing her back against the bed.

"Tell me what you want, baby. I need to hear you say it." His heated eyes bored into hers, dominant and male.

"I want you to kiss me here." She looked at him with heavy eyelids and rubbed her clit. He pulled her hand away and sucked her wet fingers in his mouth. He kept his gaze on her as he licked the wetness from her fingertips.

"You taste like summer, hot and wet." He licked every drop off her fingers. "Show me where you want my mouth."

She grabbed the back of his head and pulled his mouth down to her needy pussy. He growled. His tongued snaked out carefully licking her wet folds. He drove his tongue deep inside her.

"Yes." She arched into his face. "That feels so good."

"I could go down on you for days. And still I would want more." He teased her tender flesh with his tongue in slow and steady strokes.

She writhed underneath his mouth, holding his head close. She was going to burn up just from the feel of his tongue.

He closed his mouth around her clit and sucked hard. Haley stiffened her body exploding in to a mind-blowing orgasm sending her body shattering into a million white lights. When the tremors subsided and she finally came back into her body, she glanced down at Jayden.

Jayden smirked with male pride as he crawled up her body and between her thighs. He pressed his thick erection against her.

He ran his hand across her pussy.

"This is mine."

CHAPTER 13

*J*ayden stared down at Haley spread before him like a feast.

She'd given him something no other woman had. She'd opened herself, bared herself despite her inexperience, and pleasured herself while he'd watched.

He'd never asked a woman to do that before.

And it had been better than any fantasy he'd ever had.

Her heat was singeing him. He tensed his muscles, restraining himself from plunging into her body. It took every ounce of willpower and then some not to bury himself within her.

She stared back at him with those stunning blue eyes, a half-lidded gaze of a woman who'd just come. Yet there was more, an expectation that she wanted all of him.

"Now, Jayden."

His nostrils flared as he coated himself with her wetness and positioned himself at her entrance.

He thrust forward, entering slowly inch by inch.

He clenched his jaw and forced his eyes to stay open instead of rolling back in his head with pleasure.

"Hurry up." She arched trying to force him deeper.

"I don't want to hurt you."

She gripped his wrists. "Please, I want you. I want everything, the pain and the pleasure."

Jayden growled and thrust halfway inside her.

The pleasure of her tightness rippling around his dick made his balls tighten.

She moaned low and wiggled underneath him, trying to sink him further into her.

"Haley, you're killing me. You're going to make me come before I even get all the way in you."

"Lie down," she commanded.

He clenched his jaw.

"Lie down and let me get on top."

He'd never let a woman on top. He always liked being in control. He was a fucking werewolf. But how could he refuse when she was so fucking beautiful lying there with her blonde hair spread on his pillow and his cock halfway inside her?

He rolled over.

She straddled him, pressing down until his cock was buried halfway inside. He kept his hands tightly on her waist as she tried to squirm down further on his shaft.

She placed her palms on chest and leaned over him. She covered his mouth in a blistering kiss. He tangled his hand into her long hair and held her to him keeping her prisoner to his mouth.

When she managed to break the kiss, she lifted her hips until only the head of his erection was still inside her.

She sank down, burying his entire cock deep.

His eyes rolled back in his head as he fought for control.

"Jesus, Haley, go slow or I'm not going to last long."

She wasn't listening. She lifted off his cock and slid back

down. He gritted his teeth trying to maintain control. Her pussy rippled across his cock with every stroke sending him to another realm of pleasure.

He tried to regulate his breathing as she rode him hard, but her moans of pleasure were sending the signal to his dick to come.

He reached up and pinched her nipples.

"That feels so good." Her rhythm became faster, more frantic, and he knew she was close.

"Come for me, Haley. Come on my cock," he ordered.

Her eyes widened as she rode him faster. She sucked in a breath and she cried out his name. Her pussy contracted around him squeezing him like a silk fist. He thrust up, spilling his release inside her accepting body.

Exhausted, she collapsed on top of him. He wrapped his arms around her keeping her close.

She fit every inch of him like skin. He'd never experienced that with anyone.

He frowned. But she was young and still hadn't experienced life, like he had. He'd sown his wild oats. She hadn't.

He tightened his embrace at the thought of another male touching Haley.

She lifted her head. "What's wrong? Did you not like that?" She caressed his cheek.

He froze and looked at her like she'd lost her mind. "Are you seriously asking me that? Of course I liked it. Hell, I loved it. God, you make me feel like an old man. Maybe I need Viagra." He chuckled as he scrubbed his hand across his face.

"No, you don't." She reached down and gripped his already hardening cock. "See you're ready to go again."

He grabbed her hand and lifted it to his cheek and nuzzled her. "Yes, but you're not."

She arched her brow. "I beg to differ."

"Baby, you're a virgin and I haven't been very gentle with you. You need to rest."

She started to argue but he rested his finger against her lips.

"Please just lie here with me. Just for a little while."

She met his lips and kissed him before she settled her head back against his chest.

HALEY BLINKED and lifted her head off Jayden's warm chest and smiled.

During the night he had moved her to his side but still kept her within his arms.

"Don't move," he murmured, his blonde stubble rubbing against her cheek as he pulled her close. "It's too early."

She traced his lips with her finger. "I need to shower and make coffee. I'll bring you a cup."

"Well, since you put it like that." He smiled as he loosened his grip.

She eased out of the bed and grabbed her robe.

She blushed thinking about their night together.

She had done things that she never would have acted out.

Yet, she'd done it very willingly with Jayden watching. She shivered remembering the hunger in his eyes as he followed her every movement as she touched herself. It had been everything she'd ever wanted, but she knew what they had wasn't going to last. Jayden wasn't the sticking-around type when it came to women.

After a long shower, Haley stood at the coffeepot waiting impatiently.

"I'm shocked Barrett doesn't have a newer coffeepot." She hated waiting for the whole pot to brew before taking it out.

The shower turned on and she smiled. She imagined Jayden's naked body under the stream of water as he soaped up his muscular torso. She glanced at the coffee, contemplating skipping it and joining him in the shower.

The coffee completed its cycle and beeped. She sighed and poured a cup.

Grabbing her backpack, she headed into the living room and settled onto the couch. She took a sip of the hot liquid and set her cup on the coffee table.

She pulled out her notebook. She had a few minutes to go over some notes before Jayden got out of the shower. Might as well take advantage of the time. Since this whole stalker thing started, she could barely keep her mind on her academics. She'd been so consumed with worry that she'd fallen behind in her classes. She had a lot of catching up to do.

She frowned as she fished for a pencil in the bottom of her backpack.

Giving up when she couldn't find one, she headed into the kitchen to get a pen out of her purse.

"Good morning." Jayden came up behind her and kissed her neck.

"Good morning." She laughed at his affectionate touch.

Jayden patted her butt and headed for the coffee pot.

She smiled and stuck her hand in her bag. Her fingers brushed something wet and sticky.

What the hell?

She jerked her hand out. Fear seized her and her heart stuttered in her chest.

Her fingertips were covered in dark red blood.

"What the fuck?" Jayden dropped his cup, the glass shattering on the floor. He grabbed her hand and wrapped it in a towel.

"Jesus, did you cut yourself?"

She shook her head and ran to the sink. "No, it's something in my purse." She held her hand under the sink frantically rubbing the stains off.

Jayden grabbed her purse and open it. His eyes widened.

"What is it?"

He looked up and met her gaze.

"Damn it, Jayden, tell me what it is!"

Jayden turned and held her gaze. "I don't think you want to know."

She flipped off the faucet and grabbed a towel, wiping away the water. "Show me."

He started to shake his head, but she wasn't having it.

She was done with the fear, done with having no control, done having her life taken away from her.

She snatched the bag out of his hand and looked inside.

Nausea curled in her stomach like rotten milk and she swallowed back her revulsion.

She met Jayden's gaze. "Get it out of my purse."

"I can't get rid of it, it may have evidence."

"I don't care. Get it out of my purse. Now."

He took the purse out of her hands and walked over to the kitchen sink. He grabbed an empty white garbage bag out from under the sink. Very carefully he reached into her purse and pulled out the dead baby pig with its throat slit.

"I want the right to kill this fucker, Barrett." Jayden calmly spoke into the cell phone, despite the rage racing through his body at a volatile speed.

He was feeling anything but calm.

If it was the last thing he did, he was going to kill that motherfucker.

"Keep your head, Jayden. I need to know if the stalker actually got into the house or if he somehow got to her purse while she was out." Barrett's calm voice resonated control.

CHAPTER 14

Jayden dragged his hand through his hair. "No, if he got into the house I would have known from the security cameras. That's just not possible. He must have stuck the pig in while we were out at the bar."

"Was there an opportunity when you were distracted? Where he might have had a chance to put it in her purse. I wouldn't think he would have done it in class. It would have been too messy."

Jayden's gut sunk to the floor. He knew exactly when the stalker had messed with Haley's bag.

And it had been his entire fault.

"Yeah. Last night at the bar. I got into a fight with a guy who put his hands on Haley."

"Did you think he was the stalker? Did he threaten her?"

Jayden gritted his teeth. "Not in that sense."

"In what sense then?"

"He put his hand on her and she wasn't into him." Silence.

"So you got in a fight with an oversexed college guy in a bar because he hit on Haley. That is what oversexed college guys do."

"Something like that." Jayden gritted the words out. "Can we get back to the dead pig with a slit throat in her purse?"

"Certainly. I don't think it is a coincidence that the stalker put a dead pig in her purse versus a bird or rat or even a cat."

"Why?" Jayden frowned.

"Because she's at the University of Arkansas. She is a Razorback. I'll run the tests on the pig, but I suspect it is not your regular pig. I think it is a Razorback," Barrett murmured. "The boyfriend is ruled out. And I don't think the parents would harass her, despite being douche bags."

"Yeah, I think it's someone here, someone who is familiar with her schedule and her daily activities."

"And when you arrived and started messing with her activities and taking her out, it pissed him off. That's why it's getting more threatening, more dangerous. I think the stalker sees you as a threat to what he considers his. And he considers Haley his."

"Then that makes him good as dead," Jayden growled.

"I agree. But I want you to be careful. He may start targeting you. I'm thinking you need some backup."

"Actually we ran into Kate and Braxton. They were with us when I got into that fight."

"I'll call Braxton. If he's interested and willing I'll assign him to stay in Fayetteville with you. He's been asking for information about signing up to be a Guardian anyway. This would be a good practice for him. I'm sending Zane, Lucien and Jaxon as well. They'll be there today. They are to provide backup so you won't see them unless you need them."

"Appreciate it." Jayden sighed. "We need to catch this guy and soon. I'm not sure how much more Haley is going to be able to handle."

"If my gut is right, he won't wait much longer before he gets bold and shows himself. It's been my experience that assholes like this don't like it when they sense someone else is moving in on their property."

"He's sick and delusional. If by God, he's a Were, I'm going to want to take this before a Tribunal, Barrett."

"If he is a Were I'll grant you that request." Barrett replied. "In the meantime, keep her close and call if you get anything else."

"Will do."

"And, Jayden, do me a favor."

"What's that?"

"Call your Granny. She's been dogging my ass trying to find out where you are. No matter how many times I try to explain that your whereabouts are confidential she keeps calling." Barrett sounded more weary than irritated.

"Shit. All right I'll call her later. Preferably when I'm about to lose reception."

"Whatever. Just call."

Braxton followed Jayden out to the back deck of the house. Jayden had called him after he'd gotten off the phone with Barrett to update him.

"How's Haley?" Braxton crossed his tattooed arms across his chest and looked out across the backyard. The Were might look like a badass thug, with his tattoos and blue hair, but Jayden knew the guy had a heart of gold when it came to protecting women.

"She's trying to be strong, trying to keep it together." Jayden shook his head. "But I see through the charade."

"What's the plan?" Braxton kept his eyes ahead and let him talk. Jayden appreciated the gesture.

"Stay close to Haley. See who reacts to her, especially when she's out. The stalker will be watching, trying to find a way to get close to her." Jayden faced Braxton. "Hell, that's how he got to her purse at the bar."

"Can't blame you for that. I saw how that guy was touching her. I would've done the same with Kate. That shit ain't cool."

Jayden nodded. "I need you to be available to tail us whenever we go out. See if you can catch him following us."

"You got it." Braxton nodded toward the house where Kate and Haley were inside drinking coffee. "Kate's going back to Eureka Springs tomorrow. She has guests coming in and has to get everything ready."

"It's not those crazy writers is it?" Jayden grinned.

"Actually it is." Braxton faced him. "They are having another writer's retreat and booked the Bella Luna for a full week. If you think we need more backup we could call them in." He smiled.

Jayden snorted. "Might not be a bad idea. I bet those women might put the fear of God in that asshole." Jayden shook his head remembering when he'd first met the group of romance writers at Kate's bed and breakfast.

Jayden had gone to Eureka Springs to help Braxton when he was being hunted by the Assassins. He expected guns blazing and the opportunity to rip out a few throats. What he got was a bunch of middle-aged, oversexed women who wanted to act out their fantasies. All in the name of research for their books. Or so they said.

"Tell Kate to keep them on hand." Jayden smirked and faced the kelly green yard. He'd been surprised that Barrett kept his backyard so manicured with flower beds bursting in all colors.

There were a lot of things about Barrett that surprised Jayden.

"Don't worry. He'll fuck up. It's just a matter of time."

Jayden nodded in agreement. Yes, just a matter of time. He just hoped it wouldn't be too late.

"I want to go out." Haley looked over her notebook at Jayden sitting in the recliner.

"I don't think that's a good idea." He kept his eyes glued on the TV. The only time he looked away was to check his phone for messages from Barrett.

There hadn't been any.

Haley cocked her head. "Did Barrett say I couldn't go out of the house?"

"No. I did."

Haley tossed her notebook on the couch and crossed her arms. "Well, I'm bored. And I'm getting cabin fever. I don't want another sandwich for dinner."

"Then call for pizza."

"What if the pizza guy leads the stalker to the house?" She arched her eyebrow.

"Then I'll meet him a few streets over and pick up the pizza there."

"So you'll leave me here alone and unprotected."

Jayden pressed his lips together and aimed the remote at the TV. He clicked it off and slowly turned.

"Are you being irritating for a reason?" He stood.

"I'm not trying to be irritating, Jayden. I'm just frustrated." She sighed.

His expression softened and he sat next to her on the couch. "I'm sorry. I know this must be difficult."

"It's four o'clock. Can we not even go to the park for a walk? Anything to get out of this house."

He opened his mouth and Haley knew he was going to argue. But then he promptly closed it. "Let me call Braxton."

"For what?" She frowned.

"I want him in place for backup. He'll stay far enough away that he won't be noticed if the stalker is around. He might even be able to identify who it is."

"Did you ask Braxton for help?" Kate hadn't said anything when they were in the kitchen having coffee that morning. After the dead pig, Braxton and Kate had arrived at the house fifteen minutes later.

"Barrett did. Braxton said he was wanting to join the Guardians since his move to Arkansas. Barrett said this would be a good way to break him in to see if he can handle it, or if he's a good fit."

She nodded. Braxton would make a great addition to the Guardians.

"Why don't you get ready and I'll give Braxton a heads up."

"Okay. But where are we going so I know what to wear?"

"How about something nice but comfortable."

"Okay that I can do." She stood and he grabbed her wrist.

"Oh, and Haley, don't wear those red heels."

She frowned. "Just in case we have to run?" The thought of being chased sent a chill parading down her back.

"No. I can't seem to concentrate when you have those damn heels on. It makes me think of you naked."

The sun was just going down and the buzz of the nightlife was just starting up. As with any college town, the crowds were worse on the weekend, with students and people visiting.

Jayden held Haley close while keeping his instinct on high

alert for anything that seemed out of place. But with a crowd of college students it was hard to see anything out of place. He eyed a guy with a large red Razorback hat passing by with his group of friends.

Music wafted through the streets as people of all ages milled around.

Jayden glanced around seeing if he could see Braxton watching them. But the guy was a regular chameleon. This was saying something for a two-hundred-plus Were with sleeve tattoos and blue hair.

He'd have to let Barrett know that Braxton had his vote of confidence as a Guardian.

He glanced down at Haley who was snuggled close to his side. Her firm breast was pressed into his chest, making walking with an erection very difficult. She had one arm around his waist, her finger hooked in the belt loop of his jeans.

She looked gorgeous in a white tight skirt and fitted yellow shirt. She wore jeweled high heels that sparkled with each step she took. He'd even worn that damn pink shirt that she picked out, just to make her happy.

"What?" She caught him looking and frowned.

"I told you not to wear heels." He arched his brow.

"They're not heels, they're wedges." Her lips turned up into a pretty smirk.

He couldn't resist. He bent his head and kissed her.

When he pulled away her eyes were glossed over, the same way she looked after he made her come.

He growled.

"Maybe you were right. Maybe we should just stay home." Her raspy voice shot straight to his dick.

"We have all night for that. First I need to get some food in you." He grabbed her hand and started walking. "You're going to need all the energy you can get."

She chuckled.

"We're here." He guided her up to the steps of the cozy restaurant. He'd asked Kate where to take Haley and she'd recommended the upscale restaurant.

"Wow. This is beautiful." Haley glanced around taking in the modern but elegant layout of the restaurant with its dark interior and soft lighting. Each linen-covered table had a fresh bouquet of spring flowers in white, yellow and pink.

Jayden pulled out her chair for her to sit. He eased into the chair across the table from her. He suddenly wished he had taken her to a less swanky restaurant that had a booth and he could sit next to her.

"Have you been here before?"

"No." He reached for his water.

Haley grinned. "Dana is always complaining how she wished her boyfriend would take her here. She is going to be so jealous when I tell her."

Jayden couldn't help but smile at her enthusiasm. God, how she made his chest ache.

"I guess you miss being with her."

She shrugged as sadness crossed her eyes. "A little. She was the first friend I made when I got here. She was always trying to get me to come out to eat with her and Mark. But I would never go. Didn't want to be the third wheel." Haley glanced around and leaned across the table.

"So is Braxton still tailing us?"

"Yes and he must be pretty good. I've not spotted him since we left the house."

"Barrett will be glad to hear that then."

The waitress returned with their wine and took their dinner orders.

Jayden reached across the table for her hand. "When this is over, what do you see yourself doing?"

"I used to have this dream of opening up my own fashion line. I love clothes and all the well-known designers are located in New York or California. Why not start a designer line right here in the South?"

"That' a really smart idea. " He sobered.

"Really?" She took a sip of the chilled white wine.

"Absolutely. I mean there are a lot of celebrities that vacation in New Orleans or Charleston. I bet if you could get them interested in your clothes, you could really turn your fashion line into the next big thing. Plus if you opened a store down on the coast it would help the economy. Since Hurricane Katrina and the oil spill the coast is really hurting. You would be like the South's own celebrity."

Her blue eyes shone with excitement and then she shook her head. "I don't think I would ever live in Louisiana again."

"It doesn't have to be New Orleans. You could live in Mississippi or Alabama. Or stay right here in Arkansas. "

She caught his gaze and he could tell she was contemplating the idea.

"Well, I guess we will see what happens when this is all over. No use making plans when the future is so uncertain."

He took her hand between his palms. "You will get through this. You hear me? I won't let him hurt you. I'd die first."

"Don't say that, Jayden."

"Why? It's true. I don't want you to be afraid, anymore. I want you to think about the future."

She cocked her head. "What about you? What do you plan on doing when this is over?"

Jayden shrugged and looked away. The thought of not seeing her every day rubbed at his heart like a pebble. "I don't know. I guess I have to go on to the next mission that Barrett assigns me."

She nodded and pulled her hand away. He felt the distance between them like an invisible thread. They didn't have a future together. She'd go on and do great things, while he would continue protecting the Pack. Hell, she'd probably end up marrying someone with a law degree and have five kids.

While his future consisted of nothing more than the next mission and protecting the Pack.

*H*aley stepped out onto the sidewalk with Jayden after a magnificent dinner. She felt full and happy and content. Things she hadn't felt in a while.

"Thank you for dinner." She smiled up at him. She couldn't stop the way her heart always tugged whenever she looked at him. He was gorgeous with those intense blue eyes and blonde hair. He was even sexier when he was naked and moving over her in bed with their bodies joined.

Music floated out from the bars as they walked down the sidewalk at an easy pace. Although Jayden looked relaxed she knew better. He was constantly on alert, assessing their environment and scenting any possible danger.

"I'm glad you let me take you out. "He bent down and kissed her lightly on her lips.

Her smile slipped as she frowned.

"What's wrong?"

"Nothing." She shook her head.

"Tell me."

She stopped and faced him.

"I was just wondering about the pig."

He pulled her to a private corner of a building. "What about it?"

She shrugged. "I don't know, I guess I was wondering why he didn't leave a note this time."

"Because his notes aren't working. So instead he sent the pig to scare you."

She shook her head and wrapped her arms around herself.

"I don't know. Maybe. I guess I always thought his notes were where he held his power to intimidate me so he wouldn't hesitate to leave one along with the pig."

"Barrett had the lab do an exhaustive search on your purse and they didn't find anything. No note, no fingerprints." He'd gotten that report from Barrett before they left the house.

"He's taking it further, getting more personal. Getting closer." She grabbed his hand and they started down the sidewalk.

"Haley . . ."

A shrill of his cell phone had him halting. He pulled the phone out of his jeans pocket.

HALEY WATCHED his face change from relaxed to somber. He mouthed to her that it was Barrett on the other end.

She stepped away and turned to admire the window display at the cozy boutique. Whoever had done the display had done a great job, mixing the colors of spring into the outfit worn on the mannequin.

"Hey, you're that girl."

Hayley turned at the male voice. It was two college guys dressed in sweatshirts and jeans. Their gazes went from her back to their phone.

"Excuse me?"

"You're the girl on the advertisement." They both looked at each other and grinned. "So how much?"

"How much for what?" She frowned as her gut tightened. She glanced at Jayden, but his gaze was fixed on the ground attentively listening to whatever it was that Barrett was saying.

"How much for one hour?"

Haley whipped her head back to the two guys who were suddenly only a couple of feet in front of her. She backed up. Her skin crawled, her private space suddenly invaded.

Jayden must have sensed her fear, because he was suddenly there, stepping between her and the two guys. By this time a few more students had stopped and pulled out their phones.

They looked from Haley back to their phones.

"What's going on?" Jayden asked her over his shoulder.

"I have no idea?"

The two dudes laughed and held out their phone. "Man have you been hitting that? It says she charges by the hour."

"What the fuck did you just say?" Jayden growled so loud that Haley thought he was going to shift right in front of everyone.

"I want to know how much she charges." One of the college guys looked over Jayden's shoulder and winked at her.

Jayden punched the guy in the face. The guy fell back like a tree.

"Hey man, what did you do that for? He was just asking how much she charged. It's on the university's Facebook page of things to do." The other college guy shoved his cell phone in Jayden's face.

Jayden snatched it out of his hand. Haley peeked around Jayden's shoulder and looked.

It was the university's page with a provocative picture of

her in an advertisement for sex. Blood drained from her face as a rush of nausea washed over her.

"I never took that picture. I haven't been on Facebook since I moved here," she whispered.

"Call Braxton now." Jayden shoved his phone at her. With trembling fingers she pulled up Braxton's contact info.

"You need a little help?" Braxton shoved his way through the crowd and stood on the other side of Haley. Braxton appeared before she even dialed. "I was watching."

Jayden shoved the college guy's phone at Braxton whose face became serious.

Jayden faced the crowd of college students that were gathered and now gawking at her. "This is not Haley. And she sure as hell didn't put it on Facebook. Her account and the university's have been hacked. And the next asshole that says something to her about it will have his dick ripped off and shoved down his throat. So you need to make sure the word gets out. We clear?" The group of college students stared at Jayden wide-eyed and nodded furiously. They all quickly backed away.

"Call Barrett and tell him to get someone to check out the university's account as well as Haley's. He should able to track back to see if he can find the stalker."

Braxton kept Haley positioned between them while he dialed Barrett and Jayden stood in front of her as a shield. The group quickly dispersed.

Tears burned behind her eyes and she fought not to cry. Not now, not in front of everyone. Somehow she knew her stalker was out there in the crowd watching and waiting for her reaction. That's what he wanted. A reaction.

She would not give him the satisfaction.

Jayden turned and looked at her. "Are you okay?" She nodded, not trusting her voice.

"Let's get her outta here, man," Braxton said in a low tone.

Jayden pulled her close to his muscular chest and she sighed against his warmth and his strength, her legs threatening to buckle.

They hurried back to his car, with Braxton staying close behind them.

The temptation to cry was overwhelming. But it wasn't fear that upset her. It was anger. Anger at a stranger taking her control away.

"Fuck."

Jayden stopped short and Haley almost stumbled. She looked up and followed the line of his gaze. Right to his car.

"Oh my God, Jayden." Her stomach lurched.

"Motherfucker." Braxton added his sentiments as they all stared at Jayden's black Mustang, completely destroyed.

Every window had been bashed in, along with the hood and doors. The tires had been slashed and the black paint job had been marred with white spray paint with vindictive words like *bitch* and *whore* written for everyone to see.

Jayden spun her around and tugged her into his chest, blocking her from viewing the car.

Her stalker was now trying to hurt Jayden.

She buried her face in his chest and sobbed.

Jayden gave his report to the police as he kept his eyes on Haley. Braxton stood a few feet away and nodded, assuring him that Haley was safe.

Jayden had never wanted to kill anyone more in his life than he did right now.

He glanced over at his ruined Mustang. He'd only had her

less than two years and now she was ruined. But that's not what really bothered him the most. He was most bothered about the reaction he had seen on Haley's face.

She had looked utterly terrified.

He narrowed his eyes at the cops as they took pictures of the damage.

He wasn't sure who had called them, but he didn't like it when humans interfered in his business.

A loud rumble, like an eighteen-wheeler echoed through the near empty parking lot.

An oversized truck that resembled a tank came rumbling to halt in front of him. It looked like an RV on steroids with massive tires and bulky exterior.

The driver's door opened and Barrett Middleton climbed out. Barrett nodded in Braxton's direction before heading over to Jayden.

"I got here as quick as I could."

"Which is pretty fucking quick. We called you less than an hour ago." Jayden checked his watch.

"I was on my way when you called." Barrett cast a worried look in Haley's direction. "How's she doing?"

"Terrified. Aside from a psycho leaving her notes and a dead bloody pig in her purse, he's now moved his game up to cyberbullying her on Facebook. Now the entire campus thinks she's a prostitute for hire."

Barrett turned his glare on Jayden. "I got Zane tracking her account as well as the university's. He put a block on both accounts to prevent anyone from accessing or posting anything on her page. I also made sure to send out a warning that her account had been hacked to the entire university student body. And if they knew who did it they needed to contact the number I left."

Jayden nodded in appreciation. Hopefully that would stop

a majority of the students from harassing Haley. And if it didn't, he'd tear their fucking heads off.

"Why are you wearing a pink shirt?" Barrett sneered.

"It's not pink. It's coral." Jayden shook his head. He picked the perfect night to change his wardrobe.

Jayden arched his brow at Barrett's ride. "What the hell is that thing? Looks like it needs to be in the military."

"It's the Behemoth. It's a specialized expedition vehicle. It will go anywhere in the world, desert, jungle, mountains, you name it. Most importantly it has a space for my Harley."

"And it's here because?"

"Because I had to bring some company with me and there are not enough bedrooms in my house." Barrett's mouth thinned just as the familiar thunder of approaching motorcycles filled the parking lot.

The sound made him long for his Harley, especially now since his car was wrecked.

Jayden followed Barrett's gaze as five Harleys pulled up behind the Behemoth.

He immediately recognized his fellow Guardians, Damon, Zane, Lucien and Jaxon and another rider with the signature Harley Breakout. He would have sworn the fifth Harley was his, if it wasn't for the goofy-looking sidecar.

His gut tightened as the occupant in the sidecar took off the bug-eyed goggles and helmet, revealing gray hair and wrinkles.

"What the fuck is Granny doing here and why is she in that sidecar?" Jayden glanced at Barrett for answers.

The leader took a long-suffering breath before opening his mouth. "She wouldn't quit bothering me about where I had sent you. Plus, I needed to get your Harley to you. I figured it would be good for Haley to have someone else's company besides yours."

"Wait, that's my Harley?" He jerked his head back to the

motorcycle, his gaze running over the sleek frame.

"Yes."

"So which Guardian is riding it?" Barrett snorted.

The rider, dressed all in black leather, killed the engine and dismounted. Jayden frowned. The full-face helmet hid the identity, but he knew right away from the slender frame of the driver, that this was no Guardian. He was too skinny.

The rider pulled off the helmet and a cascade of black hair spilled out.

"Ava?"

"You looked stunned." Damon came up, shook his hand and turned his attention back on Ava.

"When the fuck did Ava learn to drive a motorcycle?"

"Apparently she'd been taking them out for a while now. Just not bothering to tell me." Damon growled.

Ava walked up with a smirk and dropped the keys to his bike in Jayden's hand. "You can thank me later."

"For what?"

"Bringing your bike." She nodded at what used to be his car. "Looks like you need an alternate form of transportation."

"It's got a fucking sidecar attached." Jayden couldn't wrap his head around that concept.

"How else was I going to get Granny here?" Ava crossed her arms as Damon pulled her close.

"How about she ride with Barrett in that thing?" Jayden jerked his finger over his shoulder.

"I tried telling her that." Barrett glared. "That woman has a hard time listening to the rules."

"Are y'all going to stand there staring or is someone going to help me get out of this contraption?" Granny yelled from the sidecar.

Ava hurried back to the bike. "Sorry, Granny." She held out her hand and the older woman took it.

"Don't rush me. I'm an old lady." Granny unfolded herself from the sidecar and climbed out. She tugged her white plastic purse out and slung it over her shoulder.

Jayden was shocked to see her dressed in jeans and a leather jacket. He'd never seen his Granny wear anything other than muumuus.

"You're not old, Granny." Damon sighed and shook his head like he was running out of patience.

Jayden inclined his head to his fellow Guardians. "You drove all the way with Granny riding in a sidecar? How long did that take?"

"We left this afternoon. We would have gotten here earlier if we didn't have to stop at every rest area for her to go to the bathroom. I swear she's got a bladder the size of a peanut."

Jayden stared at his bike and shook his head. "Dude, there's a sidecar on my Harley."

Damon slapped him on the back. "Don't worry, brother. It comes off."

Thank God for that.

"Jayden!" Granny rushed forward and pulled him into a fierce hug. She pulled back and frowned as she eyed his car.

"What happened?"

"Nothing."

"Don't tell me anything. Your car has been vandalized." Granny turned her eye on Barrett. "Is he on some kind of dangerous mission here?"

"He's always on some kind of mission, Granny. Part of being a Guardian." Barrett glared at Granny. But Jayden knew the old lady wasn't scared of her new Pack Master.

"I'm going to speak to the police." Barrett called over his shoulder and headed toward the cluster of cops eyeing their motorcycle group with suspicion.

Jayden started to say they were not going to give him any

information but to his surprise, Barrett whipped out something that looked like a badge and flashed it to the nearest cop.

The cop straightened and immediately led him over to the investigator in charge.

Jayden shook his head and made a mental note to ask what kind of badge Barrett had whipped out.

Zane, Jaxon and Lucien secured the perimeter of the parking lot. Jayden knew they were trying to pick up any lingering scent or clues the stalker might have left.

"Why haven't you called?" Granny's asked.

Guilt surged in his gut. Granny was his only living relative and had practically raised him. He wasn't sure why he hadn't called. Ever since the night of the rescue he'd been pulling back from those who cared about him, needing to protect them from the hell he'd been through.

"I'm sorry, Granny. This mission had my mind focused on other things. I should have called. I'm sorry."

Granny's frown softened and she glanced over his shoulder. "Are you sure? Would Haley have anything to do with why you are so distracted?"

Jayden shook his head.

"Why not? I see the way she looks at you." "She's too young for me. She's still in college." Those words made his throat ache.

Granny cocked her head. "And she's probably the most mature of all the girls I've seen you date." "What?" Jayden snapped his head up.

"You heard me. Those other older women were silly and were not good enough for you." Granny's gaze rested on Haley. "Now, Haley, on the other hand, seems very grounded and knows what she wants. It seems your taste in women has finally improved."

Jayden's mouth dropped. He expected his Granny to tell

him Haley was too young for him and how she needed to live before settling down.

Granny never ceased to surprise him.

Granny patted him on the shoulder. "I'll go say hello to her." Her lips quirked up in the corner. "Oh, and I need to tell her I brought her order with me." Before he could say anything, his sex toy-selling Granny ambled over to Haley and pulled her into a hug.

Braxton stood a few feet away watching over her like a mother hen while he kept his eyes on the surrounding area. Damon stood beside him talking with a stern expression on his face and those damn Oakleys. They looked quite the pair. Braxton with his blue-tipped hair and covered in tattoos while Damon sported his sunglasses and leather jacket with his long scar running down his face.

Humans probably thought they were part of some biker gang.

To Jayden they were his brothers, and he would gladly lay down his life for any of them.

His gaze drifted to Haley. Granny had her arm around Haley's shoulder while Ava said something. Whatever Ava said had Haley smiling a little.

Haley met his gaze. Did she have any idea what she did to him?

His feet had taken over and were walking in her direction, some unseen force pulling him to her. "Are you ready to go home?"

She frowned and wrapped her arms around herself in a protective gesture as she glanced over at the cops. "Can we leave yet?"

"Yeah. Barrett's here now so he'll take care of the cops." He took her hand and pulled her into his arms, not caring who saw, not even Barrett. There was no one in their universe at that moment, just them.

Haley nodded and then pulled back and looked back at Granny and Ava. "Where are you guys staying?"

"With you guys of course." Granny smiled wide.

"What?" Jayden froze.

"Barrett said we could all stay at his house." Granny hooked her purse higher on her shoulder.

"I don't think there's enough room," Jayden said too quickly.

"Sure there is." Barrett appeared out of nowhere and spoke over Jayden's shoulder. "It's three bedrooms. Plus room in the RV. It's not a bad idea to have more people around to protect Haley."

Jayden opened his mouth to say speak, but really, what could he say to that?

"WHAT THE FUCK happened to my door?" Barrett growled as he stood in front of the bedroom missing a door.

"The door was stuck," Jayden muttered and looked away.

"That's strange. As many years as I've owned this house I've never known this door to stick." Barrett arched his brow.

He knew when his Guardians were lying.

"Must be the humidity."

"It's spring. There is no humidity. Even in Arkansas."

"I'm going to find some sheets for the couch." Haley cleared her throat as she tried not to laugh.

"Look in the hall closet." Barrett kept his gaze on Jayden.

"I'll go help." Jayden quickly followed.

He didn't like it when his Guardians got personally involved while on a mission. Shit tended to go wrong when they didn't have their head in the game.

"You going to tell me what's going on?" Barrett kept his gaze on Jayden.

"It's just a door. I'll pay for it."

"I'm not talking about the door. I'm talking about Haley and you. And what's going on between the two of you." Barrett had sensed something more was going on between the two from the few phone calls he'd had with his Guardian. But he didn't have proof and he certainly had bigger issues to worry about than if Jayden was trying to get into Haley's panties.

"I don't want to see Haley get hurt." Barrett cocked his head.

Jayden's head snapped up, fierceness in his eyes. "I would never hurt Haley."

"I'm not talking about physically. I mean emotionally. I don't want you to break her heart. She's younger than you, Jayden."

"Jesus, don't you think I know how old she is?" He ran his hand through his hair. "I'm sure after this is over she'll want to get on with her life at college. She'll have her freedom and the rest of her life to look forward to."

Barrett gave him an assessing look. Jayden was clearly in turmoil. After he'd been rescued by his Guardians from his captors who had tortured him, Jayden had changed. His easygoing attitude and carefree lifestyle wasn't there anymore. Jayden might have been pulled out of hell that night, but he had brought his demons with him. He'd known the full extent of Jayden's injury from that one night in Louisiana.

"Does she know?" Barrett's kept his voice calm and quiet. Although he knew everyone kept their distance when he was having a conversation with one of his men, he didn't want the women to overhear.

Jayden frowned. "Know what?"

"How you feel about her?"

The look on Jayden's face couldn't have been more priceless. He looked like he'd been caught with his hand in the cookie jar. Or Haley's cookie jar to be more precise.

He opened his mouth and what came out surprised Barrett.

"She doesn't know I'm in love with her." He looked away, pain etched in his eyes. But Barrett knew it was a different kind of pain from what he'd been dealing with over the last few months.

"And why not?" Barrett crossed his arms. It was times like this he hated being Pack Master of Arkansas. He could deal with the fighting and the missions and all the political shit. But when it came to matters of the heart he didn't have a clue what he was talking about. And he sure as hell hoped he never found out. He made it his own personal mission to avoid being mated.

"I don't know. It's like you said, she's young, and she hasn't had time to sow her wild oats." Jayden shrugged. "I don't want to force her to commit to me when she hasn't had her full college experience."

Barrett arched his brow and snorted.

Jayden glared.

That got his attention.

"I don't think she would be interested in the 'college experience' as you put it."

"What do you mean?"

"Damon told me about when you went to college and how you had your college bucket list written out." Barrett snorted.

"So?"

"Apparently you've forgotten what you wrote."

"No I haven't."

Barrett sighed and held up his hand. He pointed to each finger as he spoke. "Go to college wearing only underwear.

Bang an ugly chick. Go to class drunk. Have a threesome. Take a piss on the street." Barrett ran out of fingers and held out his other hand.

Damon stepped up next to Barrett and continued. "Get a tattoo. Have sex in every classroom. Bang a nerd. Play strip poker with a group of sorority girls. Bang a college professor." "Okay, okay, enough." Jayden held up his hands.

"I really don't think Haley's going to be interested in banging chicks." Damon smirked behind his Oakleys.

"Or pissing in the streets." Braxton stepped up and took a drink of beer he'd plundered from the refrigerator. "She might get it on her shoes and she wears really nice shoes."

Jayden snatched the beer out of Braxton's hands and scowled.

It was the only thing he could do. They were making him sound like a total dickhead.

"I guess I remembered it differently." He grimaced and looked away, unable to meet their eyes.

"I'm surprised you remembered anything at all. You stayed drunk half the time." Damon added his two cents.

Jayden shot him a glare. And he opened his mouth. And then quickly shut it. After all, what could he say?

"That's not what I want for her." Jayden gritted his teeth.

"Good, cause that's what I don't want for myself either."

All the males turned. Haley stood there, her arms crossed and her foot tapping on the hallway runner and her expression dialed to completely pissed. "But thank you, Jayden, for trying to make decisions for my life."

"Haley, I didn't ..."

She turned on her heel and marched down the hallway.

"Glad we straightened that out." Damon slapped him on the back and walked away. The rest of the males seemed to know enough to give him some space and followed after Damon.

Jayden ran his hand down his face.

He hurried into the kitchen and ran into Ava who was eating ice cream out of the carton.

"Where's Haley?"

"She went that way." Ava pointed with her spoon toward the door leading to the deck.

"Wouldn't you like a bowl?" Jayden grinned. "There are some in the cupboards."

"Nope. I plan on eating the whole thing. No need in messing up a dish." She winked.

Shaking his head, Jayden headed out the back door. His heart lurched when he didn't see her immediately. He narrowed his eyes at the corner of the deck where the trees were overgrown.

Haley sat in a chair, her knees pulled up to her chin.

"Hey." He stuck his hands in his pocket and took a step toward her.

"Hey, yourself." He could tell by her tone that she was angry with him.

"Can I sit?" He waited until she nodded her head before he eased into the deck chair beside her. He stood and angled the chair where he was looking at her and sat again.

"I apologize if you thought I was trying to tell you how to live your life. That was never my intention." His gut churned.

She turned and met his gaze. Even in the darkness he could see her narrowed blue eyes leveled on him.

It made him hard.

"What was your intention then?"

186

"To give you the opportunity to have your freedom in college." God, even the words made him nauseated. He visualized Haley in another guys' arms, laughing and kissing and doing things he didn't want to even think about.

"And that means I need to screw everything with a penis." Jayden stood up quickly, his hands fisted at his sides. Without thinking, he snatched her up out of the chair and snarled.

"Is that what you want, Jayden?" She narrowed her gaze at him "Would it make you feel better if I fucked another guy?"

"I'll kill the son of bitch that lays his hands on you." He pulled her close, slamming his mouth across hers and thrusting his tongue in her mouth.

She moaned against his lips and he kissed her deeper.

God, he couldn't get enough of her scent of her taste

He moved his mouth to her neck where he licked the sensitive spot. He felt her hands slide up inside his shirt, her warm palms pressing into the muscle of his abs. He loved her hands and how they felt on him, insistent, demanding, urging.

"Tell me what you want, Jayden," she whispered against his ear, her breath scorching him and burning him to his very soul.

"You know what I want." He didn't want to waste his time on words.

He wanted her.

He wanted her naked. And he wanted to be inside her.

"Tell me. I need to hear it." She bit his ear.

He growled and shoved his hand down the waistband of her skirt. She was already wet. For him.

His heartbeat sounded in his ears and he couldn't hear anything but his own ragged breath.

"I want you."

CHAPTER 16

*H*aley arched her pelvis into Jayden's hand. She needed more than his fingers, she needed him, all of him.

"Jayden," she murmured against his lips as he kissed her again. "I need you. Now."

Jayden pulled back and stared at her in the dark, his eyes dilated with lust and greed. He looked deadly and dangerous and she loved it.

She loved him.

Her heart trembled within her chest at the revelation.

She reached her hand down and cupped him through his jeans.

"Jesus, Haley." He gritted out between his clenched teeth.

She loved how he responded to her touch. And how her body responded to his. With him everything was so right, so perfect.

"Where am I going to sleep?" Granny's voice screeched across the porch as the old lady opened the door and flipped the light switch on.

Haley froze.

Jayden cursed.

"Well, there you two are. I was looking everywhere." Haley smiled at the old lady from around Jayden's shoulder. Thank God, Jayden had his back to his Grandmother and she couldn't tell he was sporting a tent in his pants.

"You can sleep in the room next to the bathroom," Jayden called out. His eyes were closed and his jaw tight. Haley figured he was trying to force his erection to go down.

"The room with the missing door? I can't sleep in there.

That's Haley's room. If I sleep there, where will she sleep?" "She can sleep in my bed," Jayden spat out.

"Absolutely not. Not while I'm in the house. You two are not mated." Granny crossed her arms.

Haley slowly moved her hand off Jayden's erection. He groaned.

"I'm an adult, Granny," Jayden warned.

"And you're not mated."

"Granny…" Jayden's voice held a warning.

Haley righted her clothes and spoke. She didn't want them to get into an argument over her.

"It's okay," she whispered before stepping around him. She knew he couldn't turn around. Well, not yet.

Haley smiled at Granny. "I'll sleep in my room Granny. Don't worry."

"That's a good girl." Granny patted her arm and smiled. "Come on inside and let me show you what I brought for you.

"You brought me something?" Haley frowned and stepped through the door.

"It's what you ordered from the party." Granny led her through the room to the third bedroom where her small suitcase sat on the bed.

"My order?" Haley frowned and then her expression

changed. "Oh. My. Order." She hurried to the door and closed it. She felt her face heat with embarrassment.

Holy shit.

She was such an idiot.

"Let's chat." Granny sat and patted the bed, motioning her to sit.

Haley smiled and eased onto the bed. She hoped Granny wasn't about to give her the sex talk. She really didn't put it past the old lady.

"I see that you and my Jayden have gotten close." Granny's eyes twinkled.

"Well, he was assigned to protect me." Her throat felt like sandpaper as she tried to swallow.

Granny patted her arm. "Haven't told him you love him, have you?"

Haley jerked her gaze up to Granny's old eyes. Her face heated as she shifted her weight on the bed.

"Jayden has been through a lot, ever since that night in Louisiana when he was beaten so badly." Granny's eyes grew sad. "I had never seen him so broken, physically and mentally. But he wouldn't let me worry over him. Not my Jayden. Even with his body broken like it was, he put on a brave face."

Haley's heart broke for both Granny and Jayden. She wanted to kill the red Weres responsible for his injuries.

"But since he's been here with you, he's different. He's better. You have healed him in a way that no one else ever could." Granny cocked her head.

"But I've heard that Jayden is not the one-woman type of guy." She wasn't the type to share. It was all or nothing.

"I wouldn't listen to all the rumors, Haley. Jayden might have sewn his share of wild oats, but I think he's ready to settle down. Well, enough of that. Let's get down to business." Granny smiled and pulled out a black bag and handed it to her.

"Go on. Have a look. I need to see if you're going to like it."

She reached inside the bag and pulled out the four-inch vibrator with a curved head. It was neon green.

Granny frowned. "Is it the right color? I could have sworn you ordered electric blue."

Haley bit her cheek and tried not to laugh. The whole situation was hysterical.

"Turn it on and make sure it works."

"Right now?" She was not having this conversation.

"Yeah. That way if it's broken I can return it immediately." Granny sighed and sat on the bed. "You would be surprised how many women try to return some of the products they've already used." Granny shook her gray head. "People have no manners anymore."

A giggle slipped past her lips.

Granny's gaze was trained on the green vibrator in her hand, waiting for her to turn it on.

Haley closed her eyes and hit the button. The vibrator started trembling.

"Granny, I'm not a kid anymore." Jayden burst through the door and froze. His gaze was trained on Haley's hand. His eyes widened in terror.

Without another word he turned and hurried out of the room, pulling the door closed behind him.

Haley looked at Granny. Her lips twitched as she fought a laugh.

It didn't work.

They both burst out laughing.

JAYDEN RAN RIGHT into Barrett as he darted down the hallway. The image of Granny, Haley, and a vibrator was forever etched in his brain. That right there was true torture.

"Sorry."

Barrett eyed him and then grabbed his arm as he tried to walk away.

"I need to tell you something."

"What?" Jayden narrowed his eyes on his leader, his instincts going wild.

"I got results back from the pig in Haley's purse."

"And?"

"It had been dissected and a note was placed inside the pig."

"What?" How the hell did I miss that?"

Barrett shook his head. "With all the blood and mess it was hard to see. In fact they were internal sutures. So if you had not been looking for it you wouldn't have seen it."

Jayden sighed. He'd failed Haley by overlooking that vital piece of information.

"What did it say?" He had to know. From the somber look on Barrett's face Jayden knew he wasn't going to like it.

"It said, *I'm going to fuck you and then gut you.*"

"Motherfucker," Jayden snarled. His body trembled as he fought back the urge to shift.

"You keep it tight, Jayden." Barrett growled out a warning, his gaze lethal.

"I want to kill him."

"I know. And you'll get your chance if he's Were."

Jayden trembled. "I don't care if the fucker is Were or human. Either way I'm going to kill him. "

A tumultuous growled rolled out of Barrett's throat that seemed to come from his soul. The window shivered at the noise like a sonic boom from a jet.

"You will not disobey me. You are under my command and you better remember that! Are we clear?" Barrett glared and his eyes seemed to shift from green to yellow in blood lust before returning to their natural emerald color.

Everyone came running out into the hallway, the males with their forty-fives in hand and the females with fear in their eyes. "I got it." Jayden glared at Barrett and nodded sharply.

Barrett continued his glare, refusing to look away until Jayden finally took his gaze to the ground.

He watched the back of Barrett's boots until they turned the corner to the living room. Jayden looked up at the group that had formed.

"It's late. Everyone needs to go to bed. We've had a long day. Let's regroup in the morning."

HALEY SAT up in bed and looked at the clock.

1:00 a.m.

She had tossed and turned for the last two hours. She threw off the covers and tiptoed into the living room.

She froze when she saw Braxton sprawled out on the couch, his feet sticking over the edge. No TV for her tonight.

She sighed and headed back down the hallway toward her room. Maybe she could read a book until she drifted off to sleep. She stopped and glanced at Jayden's room. Before she had gone to bed, everyone had picked their places to sleep. Jayden in the master, she in the guest and Granny in the other guest bedroom. Ava and Damon were sleeping in the bedroom in the massive RV while Braxton slept on the couch. Barrett never said where he was sleeping.

Her mind drifted back to Jayden's room. This was the first night since they'd been together that they had not slept in the same bed.

She reached for the doorknob. Uncertainty crawled up her chest as she pushed it opened.

"Come here," Jayden's voice whispered roughly in the night air.

Her heart warmed at the sound and she closed and locked the door behind her.

"Can't sleep?" she whispered as she crawled under the covers.

"Not without you." He pulled her into his chest, his mouth marking hers and taking her to lust on a whole other level.

She heard a moan and realized it came from her. But she didn't care.

"We need to be quiet." Jayden put his hand over her lips. She stuck her tongue out, licking his fingers.

"Easy." He grazed her cheekbone with the backs of his fingers. "I want to go slow with you."

She didn't need slow. She just needed the feel of Jayden on her, around her, and in her.

"I need you slow tonight. I need to savor you." His voice held a need that made her ache.

She pulled back enough for her eyes to adjust to the darkness. His blue eyes held the same need she felt.

She pressed her lips to his and settled into his warmth. Her nipples peeked through her thin cotton shirt as she pressed against him. His hand came up her back, fingertips skidding up to rest at her nape of her neck. He palmed her neck and held her against his mouth as he tortured her with his wicked tongue.

She slung her leg across his thigh, needing him closer. She ran her fingers across his muscled shoulders and clung to him. He grabbed her thigh and turned her in one graceful flip until she was tucked underneath him.

His body pressed the length of hers, his erection pressing into her stomach. He was completely nude and she regretted that she had her pajama bottoms on.

His hands slid down her ribcage to her flat stomach. His

fingers grabbed the hem of her shirt and tugged up and over her head. It was dark, too dark for a human to see, but they weren't human. They were werewolves.

His gaze stayed on her breasts as his breathing increased. His erection twitched against her stomach. She wiggled underneath him.

"So fucking beautiful." His hands palmed her breasts, rolling her nipples between his fingers.

She arched against him, her body on fire with licks of pleasure as he tweaked her nipples with his fingertips.

"Feel good?"

Her eyes widened as she arched her pelvis against his erection. Her body cried out for release.

"Shush," he whispered and bent his mouth over a nipple. He licked and then sucked the tight bud into his mouth.

"Oh, God." Haley moaned, the sensation too much to hold in.

"I want to see you come. Right now." He moved his mouth to her nipple and sucked.

Haley bucked, her hands digging into his taut ass. He growled.

"Jayden." She arched, grinding herself against him as he pinched her nipples.

She opened her heavy eyes and looked up at him. His predatory grin was locked on her.

"I love hearing you say my name."

She ran her hands up his bare back, her nails skidding across his skin. "I need you inside me, Jayden. Now."

"You'll have me. But first I want to make you come with my mouth." He pressed his palm between her wet thighs.

"Here."

She moaned.

"Then I want to make you come when I'm buried deep

inside that tight body." He moved his mouth to her jaw and kissed as he continued the journey lower.

"And when I'm done. I'm going to start all over again." She shivered as his mouth covered her clit and sucked.

That night Jayden was as good as his word. And then some.

The next day, Jayden spent most of his time with Barrett and Damon in the Behemoth, trying to track whoever had hacked Haley's Facebook account. Whoever had done it was smart and had set up hundreds of accounts that led to false accounts. It was like a freaking family tree. Just when they thought they found an end it turned out to be related to a different person.

And they had only made it halfway through the possible people.

On top of that, CODIS still hadn't found a match for the semen that was left on Haley's note. Barrett said it could take up to a week.

Jayden knew they didn't have a week. He leaned back in the chair and ran his hand over his eyes. Visions of Haley naked and under him popped in his head.

He didn't let her get much sleep last night and he'd lost count of how many times they made love. Somewhere in the early morning hours, exhausted and sated they finally slipped into a peaceful slumber.

"How do you know he hasn't followed us here?" Damon scowled as he looked over Barrett's shoulder at the state of the art monitor.

"Because Jayden never has come the direct way home. He made sure to change his route every time they returned to the house. Also, I have cameras set up on the streetlights on either end of the street. Anytime a car that doesn't live on this street drives, by it is automatically registered and recorded and checked out." Barrett turned in his chair and eyed Damon. "What's going on with you?"

"What do you mean?" Despite the Oakleys everyone knew Damon was scowling at them.

"You seem different."

"No, I don't." Damon crossed his arms.

"I think he's put on weight." Jayden arched his brow.

"That's not it." Braxton shook his head. "I think he's had some work done, Botox maybe."

"I haven't had any fucking Botox. That shit is for girls." Damon clenched his jaw.

"You look...more relaxed." Barrett narrowed his assessing gaze on him.

"Hell yeah, he's more relaxed. It's all that sex Ava's giving him. He should be so relaxed he should be floating." Jayden snorted.

"Fuck off," Damon growled.

"Sounds like you got that territory all locked up." Jayden grinned.

"Be careful, Damon, Ava just might domesticate the badass right out of you. Then what am I going to do with you?" Barrett slapped him on the back and exited the RV.

HALEY ROUNDED the hallway corner and ran right into a brick wall of muscle named Damon.

"I'm sorry." She quickly stepped back and placed her hand over her heart before walking around him.

He grabbed her by her arm.

She looked up into the reflection of his sunglasses.

"Can I ask you something?" He let go of her arm and kept his voice low. He glanced around as if making sure no one else was near.

"Sure. Ask away." What kind of question would Damon want to ask her? The only time they'd talked was when she went to see Barrett at the Guardian's compound.

"Do I scare you?"

Her eyes widened and she laughed a little. His expression didn't change. He was totally serious.

"Oh, well, I guess if I didn't know you I might be a little intimidated." She shrugged.

"What are y'all talking about?" Ava walked into the kitchen and headed straight for the refrigerator. She examined the contents before taking out some cheese. For someone so slender, Ava sure ate a lot.

"Nothing." Damon straightened and kissed his mate before striding out into the living room.

Ava arched her brow at Haley. "He's acting weird. What did he say to you?"

Haley hesitated.

"Come on. I'm his mate. That means you have to tell." Ava crossed her arms.

"Fine. He asked me if he scared me. I hope I haven't given him that impression. I mean Damon was the one who got me into see Barrett when I started getting these notes."

"No, it's not you." Ava's expression relaxed. "I heard the other guys ragging him about how he didn't look so badass since we mated." She popped the slice of cheese into her mouth and chewed. "I think they are confusing badass with being happy." She shrugged. "I don't think Damon wants anyone to think he's a pussy."

"That's the last thing I would think." Haley lowered her

voice. "When he asked me that I thought he was talking about his scar."

Ava nodded. "I think he's more secure with it now. I told him I like it. Makes him look like a hot pirate." She cocked her head to the side and looked at the empty doorway that Damon had disappeared through. "I wonder if they make a pirate costume in his size."

"I'm not sure." Haley snorted. "Possibly. Since male strippers are built like him. Surely there's a place that makes stuff. It's not like their Granny's are making it for them."

"What are Grannys doing, dear?" Granny rolled into the kitchen wearing a muumuu splashed with yellow daffodils.

"Granny. Does your sex toy line carry outfits for guys?" Ava turned her attention to the old lady.

"Of course. What do you need?" Granny plucked a grape out of the bowl on the island and popped it in her mouth.

"You got a pirate outfit? In Damon's size?"

Granny tapped her finger to her lips. "*Mmmm*. I know we've got a cop outfit. Oh wait, we have a Blackbeard outfit. Will that work?"

Ava's eyes glazed over and she slowly nodded. "Yeah, I think that will work just fine."

"Come eat while it's hot," Granny called out from the kitchen.

Everyone stood up from the living room and piled into a line for the dining room. Jayden waited until he and Haley were alone before he pulled her into the laundry room.

"What are you…?" Her words were cut off when his mouth came down across hers.

He'd needed this all day, needed to taste her and touch her without everyone watching. He'd spent the entire day with Barrett looking at possible suspects and deleting ways into her Facebook account. Still they had to wait on the CODIS results.

He pulled back and looked down in to her sleepy eyes. "I missed you."

"I was here all day," she murmured.

"I missed being alone with you. I didn't realize how much freedom we had until everyone showed up."

"We can still spend time together." She ran her hands down his chest.

"Yeah, but I can't strip you naked in the hallway." Her eyes widened with shock and then arousal. "But I can always sneak into your bedroom." She nipped his lower lip with her teeth.

Jayden growled.

"And I bet I can sneak into the shower early enough and lock the door so no one will bother us." He went hard.

He glanced down at his watch actually contemplating if he had enough time to take her up against the wall before someone came looking for them.

"I don't think there's enough time." She winked, reading his mind.

"I want to talk to you when this is all over." He blew out a breath and pressed his forehead to hers.

"We can talk now."

He shook his head. No, he needed to give her a choice. And right now with her safety at stake she might feel pressured to choose the safe option.

"Later. I promise." He covered her lips again with his.

The door flew open and Braxton stuck his head in. "You two need to get in the dining room before Granny comes looking for you." He gaze dipped down and then back up to Jayden's eyes. "Well, at least you have your pants on. She can't get on you about that."

Haley laughed while Jayden glared at his friend.

Granny's familiar shuffle on the hardwood floor had Jayden pushing past Braxton before the old lady could say a word.

Dinner was an event of fried chicken, mashed potatoes, gravy, corn casserole, fruit salad and apple pie.

Haley couldn't remember ever having a dinner as enjoyable.

Dinners with her family were a formal event, each course served at the appropriate time.

Not here.

Here dinner was spread out at once over the entire table and everyone passed the food around. And here everyone laughed and talked and actually listened to each other.

It was completely different than what she'd grown up with.

Yet she had never felt more at home.

Everyone was almost finished eating when Barrett's phone beeped. He left the table as he answered it.

"Damon, what's the story with Barrett?" Braxton nodded at the pack master's empty chair.

"What do you mean?" Damon frowned before pulling another piece of chicken on to his overflowing plate.

"I mean no one really knows much about Barrett. Usually Pack Masters inherit the title from their father. But from what I've heard, Barrett's not even from Arkansas. And he's not been here for that long."

Damon shrugged, his sunglasses covering his expression. "I don't know. He doesn't talk to me about it. Maybe he got the job by killing the old Pack Master who asked too many questions." He pointed his fork at Braxton.

Haley grinned.

"I was wondering that myself." Ava looked at Damon. "All the Guardians always speak so highly of him, but no one talks about his family."

"That's because his family is from South Carolina, dear." Granny poured herself some coffee and picked it up.

Everyone turned and stared.

"What?" Granny shrugged.

"How do you know that?" Jayden gave his Granny his full attention.

"I have been living longer than any of you, and when you live as long as I have you make a lot of connections." She took a sip of coffee.

"So how did he get here?" Braxton leaned forward to see Granny at the end of the table.

"How am I supposed to know?"

"You're the one with all the connections." Jayden smirked.

"Maybe, but I'm not a gossip."

"Come on Granny, tell." Ava pouted.

"Maybe he killed a Were in South Carolina and his penance was to be expelled from that state." Braxton cocked his head.

"If he killed someone, the Assassins would have been sent to kill him, dumbass." Damon gave Braxton a droll look.

Braxton shook his head. "Not if his family had connections and covered it up really well."

"So why would they let him be Pack Master and put him in charge of a bunch of Weres?" Jayden took a drink.

"Maybe to fool everyone." Damon shrugged. "The last place you would put a murderer is right in the middle of a pack. It's like putting an alcoholic in a liquor store."

Haley glanced around the table at all the serious expressions.

She met Ava's gaze and the female winked, clearly amused at the males rampant ideas.

Haley spoke up. "Maybe his heart was broken in South

Carolina."

Every eye turned to her.

"I'm sorry, what did you say?" Damon wiped off his sunglasses. His disbelieving blue eyes stared back at her.

"That's good, Haley." Ava leaned forward, her eyes shining with anticipation. "Go on. I want to hear more of this theory."

"Maybe his heart was broken by the one woman he ever loved. Maybe she died in a tragic accident."

"What kind of accident?" Braxton cocked his head, interested in her story.

"I don't know." She pursed her lips as she contemplated an idea. "She died in a tragic paddleboard accident in the ocean when a shark ate her."

"Then what happened?" Granny set down her coffee and gave Haley her complete attention.

Haley glanced at Jayden who was smirking. He waved for her to continue.

"Maybe he saw the whole thing and went in after her. He managed to wrestle the shark onto the sandy beach and he ripped the shark open, thinking the shark had swallowed her whole and there might be a chance she was still alive."

Damon frowned and shook his head. "Sharks don't do that. They bite their victims and chew them up." He picked up his fork clearly losing his interest in the story.

"Maybe it's a Were shark." Everyone looked at her like she'd lost her mind.

"Let's just pretend they exist." Haley sighed.

"Go on." Jayden smiled. He was clearly enjoying her story.

"After her horrible death, he couldn't stand the torment of being anywhere near the ocean. So he went to the pack master of Arkansas who gave him a job as Guardian and upon his death made Barrett Pack Master."

"You've got a crazy imagination, Haley." Braxton barked out a laugh.

"She certainly does." Silence sliced through the room as everyone turned to the doorway where Barrett stood.

"*N*ice dinner, Granny." Braxton jumped up from the table and made his escape.

Damon and Ava followed behind Braxton.

Haley held her breath. She hadn't meant anything by her little story. She was just having fun. Barrett had been the one person to help her when she needed it. She didn't want him to think she was making fun of him.

"I guess since I cooked, you guys can clean up." Even Granny hightailed it out of the room so fast it made Haley's head spin.

Jayden pushed back his chair and stood.

Her heart tumbled in her chest. Surely he wasn't leaving her, too?

"How long were you standing there?" Jayden asked.

"I need to see Haley. Alone." Barrett's voice was calm and low and Haley didn't like it.

"Barrett, she was just joking." Jayden stepped in front of Haley.

"It's okay, Jayden." Haley stood and gave him a nod.

His face was fierce, her warrior standing up for her. "I

don't want him to lecture you about that some stupid story you made up at dinner."

"This isn't about that." Barrett kept his gaze on Haley. "I need to talk to you about your parents."

Nausea swept across her stomach. For a brief second she thought her heart had stopped.

"Are they okay? Did the stalker hurt them?"

"They're fine. As far as we know the stalker has never made contact with them. This concerns something else." Barrett cut his eyes at Jayden. "Something I would like to discuss with

Haley privately."

"Do you want me to stay?" Jayden took her hand.

"I think I better hear this alone." She didn't miss the hurt in his eyes. "I need to start facing some of my fears on my own."

He nodded once and cast a glance at Barrett before stepping out of the room.

She braced herself waiting for him to speak.

Barrett pulled out a chair for her to sit down. She sat. It struck her as strange that despite his reputation as being a lethal ruler of Arkansas, there was a refinement, a gentlemanly element to him.

Barrett eased his large frame into his chair at the head of the table.

"You're starting to scare me." Haley laughed nervously.

"Your parents contacted me. They demanded to see you." His stern gaze locked on hers.

"What?" All the air in her lungs disappeared. The last thing she needed right now was to deal with her parents.

"They didn't say why. They just said it was urgent." Barrett frowned and looked away. "I told them no."

Haley snapped her head in Barrett's direction.

"You did what?"

"I don't need them here, getting in the middle of this whole situation."

Haley wanted to throw her arms around Barrett and hug him. But something in his expression told her the conversation wasn't over.

"They went to the Louisiana Pack Master and told them I refused to let them see you. He sent some of his Louisiana Guardians to Arkansas and check things out. They went back and told the Pack Master you were staying here at my house. They know where you are."

"When will they be here?" Haley felt the blood drain from her face. The last thing she wanted to see was her parents. Not now. Not after what they had done.

"In a couple of days." Barrett looked away.

She frowned. The drive was long but not two days' worth. They must not have been in that big of a rush to see her.

"I am making them stop in Little Rock to fill out some paperwork first. That should take a good long time. I thought you needed some time to get prepared to see them." Haley looked up as Barrett stood. "I'll let you know when they are near."

She nodded, touched at his thoughtfulness. He was preparing her for their arrival. He had considered her feelings when her biological parents had not.

She cleared her throat before he walked through the door.

"Barrett?"

He turned, leveling that cool gaze at her.

"Thank you."

He cocked his head. "Oh, and Haley; Damon's right, sharks don't swallow people whole."

Jayden clenched his fists and stared out into the black night sky. He'd been waiting on the deck for Haley to finish talking to Barrett. He hadn't expected the news he got. Haley's parents were coming to see her. He didn't like it. But it didn't matter how he felt, all that mattered was how Haley felt about it.

"At least Barrett gave me a couple days to prepare." Despite her bravado, her voice still sounded shaky.

"You don't have to see them."

Haley lifted her chin. "No, I don't. I wish I could tell you that I don't care if I don't ever speak to them again. But something inside me thinks they are coming here to make things right. Maybe they realized they were wrong and are coming to apologize and take me home."

Jayden froze. Would they take her back to Louisiana? He felt like he'd been hit in the stomach with a baseball bat.

Would she do that? Go back to Louisiana?

"Maybe they just missed me." The hope in her voice was enough to make his chest ache.

He pulled her into his arms. She melted into him. He loved how she fit him, like they were made for each other. He nuzzled her hair and inhaled her soft feminine scent.

"Jayden, will you stay with me when I see my parents?"

"If you want me to, I will."

"I want you there with me." She wrapped her arms tighter around his waist.

"I'm there then. Right by your side."

The back door opened and Ava stuck her head out. "Hey, is everything okay out there?"

"Yes." Haley pulled away and smiled at her.

"Everyone was getting worried. We thought Barrett was getting onto you about how we were talking about him." Ava frowned.

"No. Everything is fine," Jayden answered.

Ava stepped out onto the porch and sighed. "Good. Now maybe Jayden can go see what's going on in the damn RV."

"Why don't you go?"

"Because they won't let me in." Ava crossed her arms. "Barrett said this was Guardian stuff only and if I happened to see some of that confidential stuff he'd have to kill me." She arched her brow. "Personally, I think they're looking at porn." Haley chuckled.

"All right, I'll go check it out." He kissed Haley on the lips and headed to the door.

"Hey, tell Damon he was right. That sharks don't swallow people whole." Haley called out just as his hand reached for the door.

Jayden laughed. "I'll do that."

"I HAD no idea Barrett had a house in Fayetteville." Ava eased into one of the Adirondack chairs on the deck.

"I know." Haley sat and looked up at the stars. "He does have a cozy little backyard."

"It looks very homey. I wasn't expecting that from Barrett. I would have thought he had a condo all stainless steel and clean lines."

Haley laughed.

"So how are you doing?" Ava glanced up at the night sky, the stars splattered across the inky backdrop of space.

"I'll be doing a lot better when this stalker is caught. Then I can get back to a normal life."

"Actually I've been wondering how you were doing since October. When you were kidnapped."

Haley looked over at Ava, who no longer seemed to be watching for shooting stars but instead was watching her.

"Okay. I haven't had time to think about it since this stuff started happening." It was the truth.

"It's like I swapped one horrible ordeal for another." Haley looked back at Ava. "You know, I never had a chance to tell you thank you."

Ava frowned. "Thank me? For what?"

"For helping find me. After I was rescued and interviewed, one of the Arkansas Guardians said that it was you who found the tube of lipstick I left on the ground. You made Damon and Jayden go back to the gas station hoping someone would recognize me and my possible kidnapper. Thank God that clerk did."

Ava shrugged. "I figured maybe a woman might find a clue that a man might overlook. It was smart using the name of your lipstick to give us a clue about your kidnapper."

"I was just lucky. I mean how many female Weres actually use the color Lethal Red and have it on them?"

"I never found out how David Jenkins managed to kidnap you." Ava's voice was soft yet probing. Haley had never talked about that night. Her parents certainly never wanted to know the sordid details. But these Arkansas Weres were better than her family. They knew how to treat one another. It was a family she was quickly becoming part of.

"You don't have to talk about it if you don't want."

Haley gave Ava a smile. "Actually, I would probably feel better if I did talk about it."

Haley settled back into the chair and stared up into the sky. "I was on my way to see my boyfriend. I had gone home to get some more clothes and was going back to LSU. Even though it was late, I didn't mind the drive. I'd driven it thousands of times. I stopped at the gas station to get gas. I had to go inside because the credit card machine wasn't working. Thankfully, I had cash."

"The clerk said that David Jenkins tried to ask you for money and you said no." Ava cocked her head.

"I did. I knew what he was, that he was a Red Were

because I could smell that stench. I didn't want him anywhere near me. I kept thinking to myself how my boyfriend was going to really be pissed if he caught the scent of another

Were on me. Especially a red wolf."

"Was he the jealous type?"

"No, he was the 'all I care about is appearance' type." Haley shook her head. "Anyway, when Jenkins left without paying for his gas I remembered just feeling relieved that he was gone. I saw how he was looking at me and it was really creeping me out." Haley wrapped her arms around herself, shivering at the memory.

"I got back in my car and made sure I locked all the doors. Once I was on the road it didn't take me a few miles before my power steering was out in my car. I pulled over, and got out, someone would drive by and help. That's when Jenkins pulled his truck in behind me. It was later I discovered that Jenkins had cut my lines that affected the power steering.

"He grabbed me and threw me to the ground. I managed to kick him in the nuts and get away, but he recovered and pounced on me, shoving me to the ground again. I remember landing on my stomach and the air being knocked out of me. There was no traffic that night. I remember praying for just one car, just one to come by. I thought if at least one car came driving by he might get scared and let me go.

"He grabbed me by my ankles and dragged me back to his truck. That's when I remembered the lipstick in my pocket. Lethal Red. I managed to stick it in the ground upright, hoping someone would find it." Haley turned and looked at Ava. "And you did. So I owe you a very big thank you."

"No, Jayden is who you need to thank." Ava shook her head. "We had no idea he had found you. He's the hero."

Haley looked back at the sky and nodded. "Yes. He is my hero. More than he'll ever know."

"Why are you in such a bad mood?" Damon glanced at Jayden as he poured himself a cup of coffee. "And why in the hell does Barrett have this old ass coffeemaker?" Damon snarled, as the percolator didn't stop when he picked up the carafe and it spilled onto the countertop.

"Barrett's a tightwad and I'm not in a bad mood." Jayden glared. Okay maybe he was in a bad mood, but he couldn't help it.

"He's got blue balls because Granny caught him and Haley in bed together last night." Braxton took out the orange juice from the refrigerator and took a drink straight from the carton. "And I'm guessing from his sour mood she busted him before anything got to feeling good, if you know what I mean."

"Fuck off." Jayden glared at Braxton before leveling one at Damon.

Damon held up his hands and smirked. "Don't look at me. I already have. Twice this morning."

Jayden rubbed his hand down his face, irritated and frustrated. Very, very frustrated.

"I hear Granny's got this toy for men. It's like an artificial vagina. Maybe she brought it and you can use it." Damon lips turned up ever so slightly.

Braxton stopped chugging and looked over at Damon. "For real? Who the hell would want that?"

"I guess someone with blue balls." Damon snorted.

Jayden growled.

"What's going on?" Barrett walked through the kitchen and headed straight for the coffee pot.

"A couple of things." Damon glanced at Jayden's crotch.

Jayden flipped him the bird.

"We were wondering why you have a coffeepot that was a hand-me-down from Jesus. And we were talking about the artificial vaginas that Granny is peddling and how Jayden needs one." Braxton reached to a plate on the island and snatched one of the donuts that Ava had brought back from the bakery early that morning.

Barrett turned and stared at all three of them in disgust. "I have no interest in talking about why Jayden is requiring an artificial vagina. And the coffee pot still works so why replace it? Now having said that I'm going to the RV where I am going to try to forget we ever had this conversation." Barrett swiped two donuts off the plate.

"And don't eat all the fucking donuts." He called out over his shoulder.

"HERE'S WHAT I GOT." Barrett leaned back in his chair in the Behemoth looking at the Guardians in front of him. It was almost evening and he'd been at the computer and checking into his contacts all damn day trying like hell to close the net around this stalker.

Damon crossed his arms over his massive chest while Braxton leaned against the counter where one of the computer monitors was set up. Zane propped his hands on his hips while shooting an occasional glare at Jayden. Ignoring Zane, Jayden sat nearby resting his elbows on his knees while he waited for Barrett to speak. Lucien was out, patrolling the street as a late night jogger.

"Haley's and the university's Faccbook hacker was traced back to a building in a small town near Shreveport Louisiana."

"So it could be someone Haley knows, like her ex-boyfriend." Braxton crossed his tattooed arms.

"No. It's not him." Barrett shook his head. "I sent someone in to check it out. That building is empty and there is no name on the deed. It is a foreclosed property. Bank owned. We think that whoever it is goes in late at night with a laptop has a mobile stick with Wifi access and that's how he managed to hack her computer."

Jayden glanced out the window. "It's getting dark now. We should have someone waiting there."

Barrett nodded in frustration. When would they start trusting him? He'd been here too damn long for this to still happen.

"I already sent Jaxon. He's there now." Jayden nodded.

"What about CODIS? We get a hit from them yet?" Damon crossed his arms and leaned his hip against the counter in front of one of the four computers on the Behemoth.

"Not yet. But I got a feeling we're getting close." Barrett looked at all his men. "And when this thing goes down I don't want any trouble."

"What do you mean?" Damon frowned.

"I mean I want this to go smoothly." Barrett held Jayden's gaze. "It seems like lately we've had anything but smooth."

"I think we do smooth takedowns all the time. I don't know what you're talking about." Damon shook his head.

"I'm talking about how when we were going in after Jayden you instigated a whole bar fight in the strip club while dressed as Spartacus."

Braxton laughed.

Barrett turned his gaze on him. Braxton quickly sobered.

"Braxton, you damn near shattered the Thorn Crown Chapel in Eureka Springs." Jayden snorted.

Barrett looked at him. "And you, I don't even want to

think what the hell you're going to do." Barrett stood. He suddenly needed a drink. Something with a very strong alcohol content.

"Zane, go relieve Lucien." Barrett met his Guardian's gaze.

Zane nodded once and silently left the RV.

"Braxton, keep an eye on the computer in case we get a hit on CODIS. I'm going inside for a while."

Braxton snorted.

Damon cut his eyes at him. "What's so funny?"

"I was just thinking about you in that Spartacus costume. Where'd you get that thing anyway?"

"It's his. Granny let me borrow it." Damon stuck his thumb at Jayden.

"Yeah, and I want it back. Do you know how much that damn thing cost?" Jayden swiveled in his captain chair.

Damon rubbed the back of his neck and looked away.

Jayden narrowed his eyes. "You do still have it, right?"

"Yeah."

"Can I have it back?" Jayden arched his brow.

"Come on, brother. Ava really likes that costume." Damon grimaced.

"What?"

"Ava really likes that costume."

"Dude, she making you wear that thing in bed?" Braxton sobered.

Damon shifted his weight uncomfortably. "Not all the time."

Jayden looked at Braxton and they broke out laughing at Damon's pained expression.

"Does she make you play the gladiator slave and she's the princess?" Jayden arched his brow.

Damon froze.

"Son of a bitch. She does. You're completely serious." Jayden couldn't help but feel a little jealous. Maybe he could convince Haley to dress up in a naughty schoolgirl outfit.

Jayden jerked his head in Braxton's direction. "Are you and Kate into dressing up?"

"Not yet." Braxton sounded way too interested in going down that trail. "I wonder where the closest costume store is in

Eureka Springs."

"You can order online." They both looked at Damon.

"You make her wear that Little Red Riding Hood costume from the strip club?

"Sometimes." A smile played at the corners of Damon's mouth.

"That was one hell of an outfit." Braxton nodded in appreciation.

Damon growled. "You two assholes better forget what she looked like in that outfit or I'll rip both your eyes out."

Jayden held up his hands. "Easy, Damon. Braxton is mated and I'm..."

"Yeah, what are you and Haley?" Braxton, the nosey bastard, had turned the conversation back on Jayden.

"I don't know. Besides, we were talking about Damon's costume not my relationship."

"Oh, so it is a relationship." Damon smirked.

"You going to mate her?" Braxton asked.

"What kind of costumes are you boys talking about?" Granny peeked her gray head inside the RV. The old woman was like a damn cat. Despite her age she could sneak up on someone before you knew she was there. Everyone suddenly found some busy work that needed their undivided attention.

The door slammed shut and everyone looked up. Barrett stood there with his coffee cup halfway to his lip. He frowned. "What are you ladies talking about or do I not want to know?" Barrett scowled.

"We were talking about if Jayden was going to mate Haley," Damon offered.

Jayden glared at the Were.

"I thought you were talking about costumes for sex." Granny shrugged. "That seems to be what the ladies were asking me about. They even wanted to see a catalogue."

Damon blinked. "You have costumes?"

"Fuck my life." Barrett threw open the door of the RV and headed back into the house.

TWILIGHT WAS QUICKLY MELTING into night. Haley stared at Jayden, listening quietly while he filled her in on how they tracked the account that had hacked her Facebook account to Louisiana. For some reason she never really expected her stalker to be from her home state and possibly someone she knew.

It just didn't feel right.

"But the building is a foreclosed property. It's not tied to anyone." Jayden shook his head. "So it's owned by the bank. Barrett is running checks on all the employees of the bank to see if anything comes up."

She nodded once and glanced away. "I don't know, Jayden. I guess I never really suspected that someone I actually knew could be doing this."

"Stalkers usually know their victims. He could be someone that you turned down for a date one time, or someone you might have gone to high school with that had a fascination with you."

"I didn't really date in high school." Her gut clenched as her childhood memories rose up. "My parents were more concerned about me keeping my grades up and getting into LSU." She tried to recall anyone asking her out but couldn't come up with anyone.

"Maybe it was someone who had a crush on you that you never noticed. Stalkers are usually the last person you expect." Jayden reached for her hand. His thumb made tiny circles in her palm.

She got shivers of a different kind this time.

Only Jayden could make her forget her worries with just one touch.

She grinned.

"What?" A slow smile played at the corners of his lips.

She stepped into his embrace and ran her hands up his muscled arms to his strong shoulders. "I was just thinking that even with all this drama going on I still want to jump you right here."

His eyebrows shot up. "Really?" He tightened his grip on her shoulders. "Out here on the deck?"

She looked behind her and then back at him. "Up against the wall in that dark corner, just in case someone walks out here."

"I like the sound of that." Jayden leaned in and growled.

"And then maybe—" Haley froze and cocked her head.

"What is it?" Jayden looked around for some hidden danger.

"That was weird. I thought I heard my mother's voice." She looked at Jayden. "But that can't be. Barrett said it would be at least tomorrow before they arrived in Fayetteville. We were going to meet in town since they didn't know the address of the house."

"Let's go see." Jayden headed inside with her following closely behind.

Jayden came to a stop, forcing Haley to run into his back just as they came around the kitchen.

"I demand to see my daughter." The familiar voice of her mother echoed through the kitchen.

Haley peeked around Jayden's back. Her parents were in the kitchen dressed like they were going to the ballet and addressing the Arkansas Pack Master. Braxton and Damon stood on either side of Barrett in a defensive posture. Her parents' backs were to her.

Jayden reached behind her holding her still.

"You are in my territory now, lady. And I strongly suggest you get your finger out of my face." Barrett's voice was even but the undercurrents of rage were audible.

"Do you know who we are?" Her father, John Stanley Guthrie III, puffed out his chest and moved closer to Barrett.

Barrett glared down at her father and Haley was astonished at the difference in height. She knew Barrett was tall, but she didn't realize just how tall until now.

"I know who you are. Let's be clear, that shit doesn't mean anything here. Here, I am Pack Master of Arkansas. Here, I am the Law. Here, you are nothing," Barrett growled.

Haley gasped. She doubted anyone had ever spoken to her parents like that.

Everyone turned. For the first time, her parents noticed her standing there.

Their eyes widened and she expected them to run forward and pull her into their arms. She expected them to tell her they were sorry and that they missed her.

"What have you done, Haley?" Her mother turned to face her with a look of utter disdain. Haley jumped back, as if she'd been slapped.

"Is it not enough that you ruin yourself with that red wolf? But to publically disgrace our family name by advertising yourself as a whore on Facebook in order to retaliate against us?" Her father's face reddened and his narrowed eyes made her feel like she was looking at a stranger.

The room went silent. Granny and Ava were standing by the refrigerator with their mouths hanging open. While Barrett and his Guardians were snarling, their teeth bared.

And then there was Jayden. A slow torturous growl emerged from deep in his throat. Her father and mother both jumped back, their eyes wide with either fear or the fact that someone actually growled at them.

"You are both the most pathetic excuses I've ever seen for parents." Jayden pointed at them.

Her parents' mouths dropped open. Haley held her breath.

"Your daughter was kidnapped yet you blamed her. And when she is brought back to you, safe and unharmed you're devastated because people will assume she's been raped and ruined your reputation." Jayden took a step closer.

"And now when a stalker hacks her Facebook account and spreads vile lies about her, you still blame her. You are both pathetic and if you ever dare say another harmful word to her or about her or look at her wrong, so help me God, I'll end both of you and no one will ever know what happened to you."

Her father turned to Barrett with a smirk. "Your Guardian just threatened me. I insist on immediate discipline and for him to be removed from his position."

"You're going have to file a formal complaint," Barrett growled. "But before I can render my verdict, I'll take into consideration that you ignored my direct orders about going to Little Rock and filling out paperwork to request a meeting with Haley. I'll also remember how you defied my orders of meeting tomorrow in town. After that, I will be sure to wipe my ass with your fucking complaint."

Ava snorted and clasped her hand over her mouth.

Her mother glared at her but apparently knew enough not to say anything.

Haley fought the urge to smile. She'd never seen her parents so nervous before in her life. They made a habit of making other people squirm and now they were the ones in the hot seat.

"Now, if you want to see if Haley is willing to talk to you, then I suggest you ask, nicely. Otherwise you both can get the fuck out of my house." Barrett stepped into her father's space daring him to speak.

"But…" Her father made the mistake of opening his arrogant mouth.

"And Damon and Braxton will be glad to show you the door." Barrett smiled, his white teeth glinting like shark's teeth. Braxton and Damon stepped forward.

"Barrett, it's okay. I'll listen to what they have to say." Haley stepped away from Jayden. She felt his hand at the small of her back for support. She gave him a smile.

"And whatever they have to say can be said in front of everyone here."

CHAPTER 18

"*I* think it would be best to speak privately, Haley." Her mother lifted her chin.

Haley shook her head. "No mother. They're my friends and they have been a better family to me than the two of you. So I suggest you tell me what you want so you can leave." Her heart ached at how bad things had gotten between them.

"I think you need to tell us what's going on with this Facebook thing," her father ordered.

"What is there to tell? Someone is targeting me and has hacked my Facebook account."

Her father looked stunned. He glanced around the room and nodded at Jayden.

"He said something about a stalker. What is he talking about?" Her father's cheek muscles twitched and she knew it was taking all the patience he had to control his tongue. Her father was not a patient man nor was he used to people not snapping to attention when he wanted something.

"When I moved here I started getting notes. They started out harmless but became quite aggressive. So I went to

Barrett since he is my new Pack Master, and asked for his help." She glanced at Barrett who was still holding his dominant posture. If they so much as touched her she didn't doubt he would intercede. If Jayden didn't beat him to it.

"I see." Still her father showed no emotion.

"Now why don't you tell me how you found out the address to my house?" Barrett glared at her father who blinked rapidly.

"The Louisiana Pack Master gave it to me. He said he stayed here one time when LSU was playing Arkansas." Barrett's eyes flashed yellow with blood lust. He was clearly surprised that the Louisiana Pack Master had given out that information. Haley knew that whatever business had transpired between the states and their alpha leaders was top secret. But she also knew that Louisiana's Pack Master was quite manipulative when he wanted something.

"I see. Tell me, how much money did you have to pay him to disclose that information?"

Her father's face grew red. She knew immediately her father was guilty of bribing the Louisiana Pack Master.

"I'm sorry, Barrett," she whispered. She had never been so ashamed of being related to her own parents as she was at that moment.

"You have no need to apologize, Haley. Your parents have put you in grave danger by coming here. And if they led your stalker here and endangered your safety I will make sure to exact my punishment as Pack Master of Arkansas."

Haley's stomach dropped.

"What do you mean, 'endangered Haley'? We would never intentionally do that." Her mother put a trembling hand to her throat, her diamond rings sparkling in the light.

"Don't worry. I have no doubt that the stalker knows my parents have disinherited me. They would never suspect they have come to see me." She felt Jayden step closer behind her and she drew her strength from his warmth.

"Whatever you saw on Facebook, you can be assured I did not put it there. So you can tell all your socialite friends it was hacked."

"Well, what did you expect after that episode in October, when you were...ruined?" Her father's voice dropped on the last word.

THAT WAS IT. Jayden had forced himself to stand quietly by and listen to Haley's parents' bullshit for far too long. He should have shut them up when he saw them.

"Ruined?" Jayden's entire body trembled with uncontrollable rage. "Is that how you see your daughter?"

"You are so blinded by what other people think. Haley is not ruined."

"Jayden, it's okay." She touched his arm and looked up at him. But he knew better, she wasn't okay. She was crushed by her parents. It pissed him off.

"No, baby it's not okay." Jayden looked up and caught Ava giving him a soft look as she cooed, as if she were watching a Hallmark commercial.

His gaze landed on her parents.

"What happened in October was never her fault. She was kidnapped and held against her will. And she was rescued and brought back to you unharmed."

"She was not unharmed." Her mother's lips pressed into a thin line.

"Actually I was. Jayden came into the room before that red

Were raped me. Jayden killed him."

"But..." For once her mother was at a loss for words.

"Why didn't you tell us?" her father demanded.

"You never gave me the chance. I tried to, but you both said you didn't want to hear anything I had to say. I knew that night I was dead to you." Her voice wavered.

"Haley, this means you can still marry Anthony. And you can come home to Louisiana." Haley's mother's face brightened immediately with relief.

"Yes. Go get your things and we'll leave immediately. I'll call the dean and have him transfer your records back to LSU first thing tomorrow."

Haley stiffened. And then she pushed his hands away and walked right up to her parents.

"You're kidding me, right?"

"No. You can come home." Her mother smiled.

"I tell you what you can do. You can both get in your car and go home. And don't bother trying to contact me again. If you do, I'll talk to Barrett and have him put a restraining order on you, barring you both from ever entering the state of Arkansas again."

"Haley Guthrie, don't you dare talk to us that way. We're your parents," her father snarled.

She shook her head, her face pale and eyes disbelieving.

"No, you're not. Not anymore." She walked past them, and Barrett and his Guardians parted, letting her through the living room.

"Don't you do this, Haley. There are no more second chances," her mother called out in desperation.

Haley turned. All eyes on her. She looked straight at her mother.

"You're exactly right, Mother."

THE ROOM ERUPTED into chaos as Haley walked out the door.

Jayden was threatening to beat her father's ass. Braxton was trying to keep Jayden from getting within hitting range of the dad, and Damon was looking like he was ready to jump in and get his punches in after Jayden. Even Granny and Ava ganged up on her mother, telling her what a poor excuse she was for a parent.

Barrett blew out a breath just as his phone rang. He reached in his pocket and headed into the living room to answer it.

"Hang on. I can't hear a fucking thing." Barrett headed into the back yard.

"Okay. What do you have for me?" Barrett strained to hear what Jaxon was telling him. He frowned as he repeated the information back to him.

He hung up.

He ran into the house and yelled. Everything went quiet.

"Damon, go check and see if CODIS has a hit," Barrett commanded.

Damon hurried out without a word.

"What is it? What's wrong?" Jayden turned his attention to him.

"Jaxon called. He said there was a picture taken of a guy who tried to enter that building this morning where Haley's account was hacked."

"And?"

"And he's running the tags on the car." Barrett looked around the room. "Where is Haley?"

"I thought she went out to the backyard." Jayden paled.

"No. I just came from out there." Jayden hurried out the front door. A few second later Damon entered the kitchen with a paper in his hand.

"CODIS has a hit." Damon held out the paper.

Barrett snatched the paper and looked down. He blinked.

"You look like you know him, Barrett?" Braxton slid closer "This isn't possible." Barrett shook his head.

"Who is it?" Damon glanced down at the photo.

"It's the guy that tried to rape Haley." Barrett looked up.

"But Jayden said he killed him."

Jayden ran back into the house. "She's gone."

Jayden look around at everyone. "What is it? Has there been a hit?"

Barrett nodded and held out the picture of the attempted rapist.

Jayden's eyes grew wide and he shook his head. "That's impossible. I killed him. I broke his neck."

HOT TEARS BURNED her cheek as Haley ran down the sidewalk. She needed to get away from all the hurt and pain her parents had caused her.

Humiliated and embarrassed, she just wanted to hide from everyone and everything. She glanced behind her slightly shocked and pained that Jayden hadn't run after her.

She slowed down when she got to the corner and wrapped her arms around her stomach.

She turned the corner.

"Haley!"

She froze as a truck pulled up to the corner.

"Mark. What are you doing here?" She walked over to his window.

"Hey, are you okay?" His concerned voice helped her relax.

"Yeah. I was just out for a walk." She wiped the tears from her cheek and glanced away. "What are you doing here?"

"Dana's been trying to call you. She really needs to talk to you."

"What's wrong?" Her stomach lurched.

"She wouldn't tell me. She said she only wanted to talk to you."

"Okay. Let me go back to the house and tell everyone where

I'm going." She stepped back

"Jump in and I'll drive you down, then we'll go over to Dana's." He reached across the truck and opened the side door.

"Yeah. Okay." Haley climbed in.

Mark drove down the street and took a right onto the main road. He gave her a sheepish smile. "I promised to pick up some flowers from the florist before they closed. Then I'll take you home."

Haley frowned.

"Just a quick detour. I promise."

"Okay, but hurry."

JAYDEN PICKED up his cell phone and dialed Haley's number, praying she had taken it with her.

Ava came running into the living room holding a ringing phone.

"It's Haley's. She didn't take it." Jayden disconnected and shoved his phone back in his jeans pocket.

Barrett burst in from the front door with Damon and Zane right behind him. "I checked the surveillance video from both ends of the street. It looks like Haley got into a truck with a male."

Jayden snarled. "What did he look like?"

"Hard to tell, he had a baseball cap on and his face was in the shadow," Damon offered up.

Haley's phone rang. Everyone looked at Ava. She looked at the caller ID. "It's from a Dana."

"Give it to me." Jayden answered the call.

"Dana."

"Jayden, why are you answering Haley's phone?" Dana's voice sounded shaky.

"Because she's not here. Is she with you, Dana?" Jayden knew he sounded sharp, but he didn't' really care. He needed to find Haley.

Dana inhaled loudly. "No. That's why I was calling. I really need to talk to her. Mark told me something today that is very upsetting and I …" She broke off into pitiful sobs.

"What? What is it? Dana, this is serious. I really need to know." Jayden was aware that every eye in the room was on him.

"Mark broke up with me."

Jayden fought the urge to roll his eyes. Haley was missing and this girl was upset over a breakup. "Sorry to hear that."

"I know! He said the reason he was breaking up with me was because there was someone else." Dana started up the water works.

"Dana…"

"He said he's in love with Haley."

Jayden froze and every sound went mute. It was like someone had turned off the volume.

"What?"

"He said he's in love with Haley. Did she ever say anything to you? I don't understand how this could happen."

Jayden walked over to the coffee table and snatched up the photo of the Codis hit.

"Dana. What's the name of your boyfriend?"

"You mean ex!"

"The name, what's his name?"

"Mark Boulland."

Jayden let the phone slip out of his hand. Someone must

have caught it before it hit the floor because he was vaguely aware of Ava speaking to Dana.

All he Jayden could see was the name at the bottom of that white piece of paper. Mark Boulland.

"SHIT. He was hiding in plain sight. The whole fucking time. He was a student at the same university as Haley, yet I didn't see him." Jayden loaded every weapon he had into the RV. The plan was to shift in to wolf form and sniff out Haley's scent while the RV followed. They would then weapon up once they were in human form again.

"Sociopaths usually are pretty fucking genius. We miss them all the time. Don't beat yourself up about it." Damon slapped him on the back as he walked through the RV checking out any updates from satellite images as to where Haley might be.

Ava boarded. "Okay, here's what I got. Dana said Mark has a cabin near the lake. She's only been out there one time and it's pretty isolated. Here's the address. She handed it to Braxton who punched it into the RV's Navigation. An address popped up.

"I also told her if Mark calls her to be sure to let me know." Ava slid her cell phone back in her pocket.

"I'm repositioning all our satellites within a hundred-mile radius. " Barrett punched in some kind of code on the keyboard of the computer and automatically aerial pictures popped up on the screen.

"We have satellites?" Braxton murmured to Damon.

"Apparently." Damon nodded in appreciation.

"Just give me the coordinates." Jayden clenched his fists as rage filtered into every cell of his body.

"Hang on." Barrett shifted through some pictures as Damon cross-checked the addresses.

"Come on." Jayden narrowed his eyes, trying to force the damn computer to hurry the hell up.

"I said wait. If you bust up in the wrong fucking house you are only going to waste time getting to Haley." Barrett cut his eyes at him.

Jayden gritted his teeth.

Barrett was right. He knew it. But all that mattered to Jayden right now was getting Haley back safe and sound.

HALEY SHIFTED in the front seat of the beat-up Ford truck. She hadn't noticed the smell when she first got in, but she was no longer able to ignore the stench.

"I didn't know you had a truck, Mark. I've only ever seen you drive your Prius." She swallowed and tried breathing through her mouth. Maybe he'd hit a skunk.

Mark's cheek twitched as he stared straight ahead. He continued on the street and then turned onto the highway.

"Hey, you missed your turn for the florist." Haley turned in her seat as the lights of the city disappeared behind them.

He shook his head. "Change in plans."

Dread, like skeleton fingers, scraped down Haley's spine. She turned and faced him. "Okay. Well, I still need to go back and tell Jayden where I'm going. You can take this exit up ahead."

This time when Mark looked at her, his eyes were empty and hollow. "No. I'm not taking you to Jayden. You are mine. You always were."

Haley's stomach bottomed as terror careened through her system. She reached for the door handle and pulled.

Click.

She froze. The unmistakable sound of a gun being cocked clenched her muscles to the point of pain.

"Don't do that, sweet Haley. I'd hate to kill you before we've had our time together."

"HURRY." Jayden stood over Braxton's shoulder as he maneuvered the Behemoth on steroids down the back roads that led to the cabin. The Behemoth's big tires made light work of the uneven terrain.

"I'm going as fast as I can. The road's getting narrower," Braxton gritted out.

"I'm out." Jayden ran for the back door only to be caught by Barrett's massive hand. He glared at Barrett. "You're not stopping me."

"I didn't plan on it. According to the satellite images we are only a mile from the cabin." Barrett narrowed his eyes on Jayden. "I have no idea what we'll be walking into so we need to exercise caution."

"I want to take the lead." Jayden's heart thudded in his chest like a tiger trying to claw its way out of a cage.

Barrett cocked his head and nodded once. The RV pulled to a hard stop.

"We're officially out of road." Braxton put the Behemoth in park and came into the back with the rest of the werewolves.

"I want everyone weaponed up."

"But I can get there faster if I shift." Jayden shook his head determined to do whatever it took to get to Haley.

"If you shift there's no way to carry your guns."

"I got an idea." Damon walked over to a black duffel bag and pulled out what looked like a harness.

"Ava had it made for me. It's a gun holster. Once Jayden shifts, I'll strap it on him with his weapon. Once he gets to the cabin he can shift back into human form and use it." Damon shrugged.

"And he'll be buck ass naked." Braxton frowned.

Jayden opened the door of the RV and hurried out, pulling off his clothes as he went. "Let's do it then." He closed his eyes and called to his inner wolf. His muscles stretched and his ligaments lengthened and shifted, while hair covered his entire body

Jayden opened his eyes and growled. He walked up to Damon.

"All right, Jayden. Remember, once you shift back into human, this is not going to fit so it will fall off. Make sure you shift before you engage the stalker." Damon snapped the harness/holster around his wolf body and stuck in a .45 Sig Sauer.

"The coordinates are a half mile through the woods." Barrett put his hand on Jayden's neck to make sure he was listening.

"We'll be right behind you, armed. So you need to wait until we get there. Just assess the situation and text it back to me." Barrett grabbed Jayden's cell phone out of his jeans lying on the ground and tucked it securely into the gun holster.

"We clear, Jayden? You don't make a move until I say." Barrett glared down at him.

Jayden nodded once.

He would feel Barrett's wrath later when his Pack Master discovered he lied.

HALEY SLOWLY WALKED toward the cabin door. She knew the second he got her inside he was going to rape her.

And then God knows what.

She needed to buy time. Surely Jayden would be looking for her by now.

"Move it." The metal of the gun stabbed her in the back

while Mark growled. "Don't make me shoot you and drag you inside."

She gasped.

He laughed softly, the sound raking across her skin like death.

"There are lots of places for me to shoot you Haley and still be able to enjoy you."

He reached around her and turned the knob and pushed her through it.

Her foot caught on the rug and she stumbled to the floor. He cut the light on, flooding the cramped space with light.

The cabin was one big room and rustic. The kitchen was located behind her while to her left was a living room with a nasty-looking couch and a fireplace along the wall. Steps along one wall indicated a second level.

He followed her eyes to the second level loft and looked back at her. "Yes, the bedroom's up there. We'll be spending a lot of time there."

"Why are you doing this? What about Dana? You were supposed to be engaged." Haley got to her feet and stood, not taking her eyes off Mark.

"Because of what happened in October." He cocked his head.

"How do you know about that?" Holy shit was he one of the kidnappers? Cold fear flooded her veins.

His face grew grim. "I knew about the kidnapping. In fact my brother told me they were planning to take you and wanted me in on it." He shook his head. "But I said no. And then Jayden comes along. That motherfucker killed my brother. Broke his neck." Mark's eyes shifted to yellow as he snarled. Haley felt the blood drain from her face. It all hit her at once. Mark's scent, his familiar face. She had only caught a glimpse of her potential rapist before Jayden came in and killed him. It had been dark and she'd been so scared that she hadn't really paid attention.

"He was your brother?"

"Yes." Mark glared at her. "My twin."

"But, how did you … I mean, I would have recognized your…."

"My scent?" He chucked darkly. "I camouflaged my scent on the rare occasions I was around you."

"But wouldn't Dana have recognized your scent?" Red werewolves had a very distinctive odor.

"You'd be surprised how much a desperate female will overlook." Mark arched his eyebrow. "Besides I made sure to spend a lot of time in the cadaver room. The scent of formaldehyde covers just about every kind of smell you can think of." Haley swallowed the lump in her throat.

"But, Mark, you were going to be a doctor. And doctors help people. Not hurt them. You still have time. Just let me go."

Mark gave her a look of amusement. "That's sweet. You have this all figured out in that pretty little head of yours."

His amusement faded. "It's not that easy. It never is. It didn't start out this way, you know. I started following you after you left LSU. It seemed to fill the void left from my brother. I really did love you, Haley."

"Did."

She swallowed.

"It changed when Jayden entered the picture. If you had just kept quiet I would have been able to court you, to make you feel what I feel about you. I knew you were untouched, still a virgin." His gaze hardened. "But you had to go and tell Barrett. And he assigned my brother's murderer to guard you." Mark looked up, the muscle in his cheek twitching. "Do you know how much that hurt seeing you with him? With the one who killed my brother?"

"Mark, please…" Haley backed up a step, her mind going a million miles a minute. She didn't have any more time. She was going to have get herself out of this mess.

"If you had just waited, but no, you listened to his lies and let him touch you." His hand clenched around the gun and his free hand hit his upper thigh in a rhythmic motion.

"You shouldn't have been such a whore, Haley. Maybe then I could have loved you again. And now you don't give me a choice. After I fuck you I'm going to send you back to Jayden in pieces."

CHAPTER 19

*J*ayden shifted back into human form the second the cabin came into view. He grabbed the gun out of the holster and dialed Barrett as he ran toward the house.

"I'm here." He hung up. He had broken protocol by disobeying Barrett's orders to wait. He'd deal with the fallout of that later.

If there was a later.

The scent of red wolf stung his nose as he passed the piece of shit truck.

He heard Haley's voice and held his breath as he leapt onto the porch and shoved his way through the door. Wood splintered and groaned as he went straight through the fucker.

Mark turned, clearly startled before leveling the gun at Jayden.

Jayden rushed him, tumbling them both to the floor. Jayden's gun skidded across the floor. Haley screamed and then a gunshot rang out. He tightened his grip around Mark's hand and shoved the gun across the room.

He glanced up to make sure the bullet hadn't hit Haley. She stared back at him with terror in her eyes, her face as white as a sheet.

"Haley, are you okay? Are you hit?" He wanted to go to her, but he couldn't let go of Mark

"Jayden," she whispered. She pointed at him.

He glanced down into Mark's face thinking he'd killed the other brother as well. Instead of a death mask, Mark was smirking.

Jayden frowned.

"How's this feel?" Mark punched Jayden right in the gut. Pain rippled through him, white-hot and fiery. Jayden looked down at the blood across his abdomen.

He'd been shot.

Jayden held back his groan. He tightened his grip on Mark.

"Haley, get out of here. Now!" Jayden screamed. He had to make sure she was safe.

Mark grinned and dug his finger inside the gunshot wound. Jayden grabbed his arm, but his hand was slick with blood and he slipped out of his hold. Mark arched and tossed Jayden off him and stood.

Jayden grabbed his side and stood, keeping himself between Mark and Haley.

Mark laughed. "This is perfect. You get to watch me fuck her before I kill her. What do you think about that, asshole?"

A feral growl erupted throughout the cabin shaking the windows.

Jayden thought at first it was Barrett coming in from behind him, but a sudden dizzying flash of petite gray fur had him rethinking.

ANGER PULSED through Haley the moment Mark shot Jayden.

She was tired of being afraid, tired of not living, tired of not taking chances.

No more.

She shifted into wolf and took back her power.

And then she lunged. She used all her weight to shove Mark back. His head hit the floor with a sickening thud.

She arched and sunk her teeth into his crotch.

Mark screamed and tried to buck her off. But she wasn't letting go. Her jaws were locked down. Blood seeped into her mouth fueling her anger.

If Jayden died, so would Mark.

BARRETT RUSHED AHEAD of the Guardians just as Jayden ended the call. He knew what Jayden planned on doing and it was going to damn well get him killed.

Barrett ran into the cabin, weapon drawn, and then came to a halt.

Damon was right behind him with Braxton on his heels.

Their stalker was screaming like a pussy as Haley had her wolf teeth buried in his crotch.

"Damn," Braxton muttered and paled a few shades.

Barrett's gaze landed on Jayden, lying on the floor, blood pooling around his side.

"Braxton, go get the medical supplies." Barrett rushed to Jayden's side. Barrett tugged his black tee shirt over his head and pressed it against the gunshot wound.

"What about Haley?" Braxton muttered.

"I think Haley's doing just fine." Barrett barked out. "Go now!"

Damon came around to Jayden's other side and Barrett could see the worry in his face. The two males had been raised together, like brothers, before fate had taken them down different roads. But like life, they had once again found each other.

"Jayden, you better not fucking die on me." Damon whipped off his Oakleys and grabbed Jayden's hand. "If you do I'm going to set Haley up on a date with Jaxon."

Jayden's eyes cracked open a little and he grimaced. "And I'll fucking rip your throat out, wolf."

Barrett breathed out a sigh. "Now, now, children. There will be plenty of time to fight later."

"What about Haley? Is she okay? Is she hurt?" Jayden made a weak attempt to sit up. But Barrett pressed him back to the floor.

"She's fine. She's probably bitten off Mark's dick by now." Damon grinned.

"Well, damn. Get her off him." Jayden's pale face grimaced.

"She doesn't know where that's been."

Damon looked to Barrett. Barrett nodded his okay.

"Haley, it's okay. You can let go now." Damon's voice was calm. It always amazed Barrett how such an aggressive warrior like Damon could speak so calmly.

Still, Haley kept her jaws locked on Mark's crotch. Barrett almost felt bad for the guy.

Almost.

"Haley, Jayden needs you." Barrett fixed his gaze on Haley while his hand pressed his shirt against Jayden's bleeding wound.

Her wolf eyes met his and held. She blinked and then let go. She trotted over to Jayden and sat. She placed her head on his neck and whimpered.

Jayden grinned and rubbed her head, his eyes opening. "You still look hot, sweetheart." He coughed and blood sputtered out of his mouth.

Barrett gritted his teeth. "I got to roll you over Jayden. I need to see if the silver bullet is still in."

Barrett didn't wait for him to understand. He didn't have time.

Damon squatted by Haley and wrapped his arms around Jayden's side. He waited for Barrett's signal. He turned Jayden on his side.

Jayden groaned. Haley whimpered.

Barrett ripped Jayden's shirt in two and grimaced at what he saw.

Barrett looked at Damon.

"Fuck." Damon cursed.

Barrett reached in his holster and pulled out a knife. It wasn't sterile, but Jayden would heal from the cut. But if the silver bullet stayed inside, he would slowly die.

"Haley, shift. I need you to help Jayden while I get the bullet out." Barrett narrowed his eyes at Haley.

Barrett averted his eyes as Haley trotted to the corner of the room and shifted. When she returned to Jayden's side, she had a quilt wrapped around her naked body.

"You ready?" Barrett held her gaze.

"Yes." She leaned down, her face only inches from

Jayden's. "This is going to hurt. Scream if you want to, okay?" Jayden chuckled. "I won't make a sound."

Barrett gritted his teeth. What he was about to do wasn't going to be painless. Barrett glanced up at Damon. "Do we

have any kind of painkiller? Alcohol?"

Damon shook his head.

Braxton burst through the door, the medical satchel in his hand. "What do you need?"

"Any morphine in there?"

"Yeah, right here." Braxton pulled out a syringe and bottle. He drew up something in a syringe and eyed Barrett.

"Give it to him," Barrett ordered.

Braxton stuck Jayden in the thigh with the filled syringe and pushed the plunger.

"I have to get this out, Jayden. Try to be as still as possible."

"I won't move, my alpha leader." Jayden's voice was eerily reverent.

Barrett knew Jayden wouldn't move no matter how painful it was.

Barrett stilled himself and positioned the knife. Jayden's body would burn off the effects of the painkiller due to his high metabolism, so he had to act quickly. He prayed the painkiller would at least dull the sting of the knife.

He cut into his lower back and Jayden flinched underneath his fingertips yet didn't cry out. Barrett could feel the bullet and wasted no time in digging his knife further into his Guardian's back.

When he finally dug out the silver bullet, he pressed a wad of gauze against Jayden's back that Braxton handed him.

After he patched the gauze to Jayden's lower back, Barrett helped Damon turn him.

Jayden's face was paler than Barrett had ever seen and he was a little afraid that Jayden might have lost too much blood.

"Is he going to be okay?" Haley looked up at him, her eyes watery.

"Yes." He hoped he wasn't lying.

Jayden opened his eyes.

Nope it wasn't a dream. He'd hoped the pain he felt was part of a nightmare. No such luck.

"Hey. You're awake."

He jerked his head toward Haley's voice. She leaned down over his bed.

"Hey you." He reached up and cupped her cheek.

"How do you feel?" Her eyes were red from where she'd been crying.

"Like I've been shot."

She smiled a little. "You were."

Jayden grimaced. "I think I remember Barrett digging out the bullet."

Haley nodded. "He did a good job though. The Guardian doctor said you should heal within a few weeks."

Jayden frowned "How long have I been out?"

"Only a day."

"Where's Mark?" Anger raged through his veins.

She looked away.

"What? What is it? Did he get away?" Jayden bolted up in bed and grimaced when his back ached in pain.

"No. He's not going anywhere." Haley bit her lip. "He has to recover from surgery." Jayden frowned.

"Let's just say he is one nut short." Haley blew out a breath.

"You bit his nuts off." Jayden frowned.

"Just one. He's still got the other."

"Well, did you wash your mouth out?"

Haley laughed. "Yeah."

"Good, then come kiss me."

CHAPTER 20

"*A*re you ready?" Jayden crossed his arms and leaned against the kitchen door. It had been four weeks since he'd been shot. It only took him a week to heal from the silver bullet. Haley had stayed by his side refusing to leave for a minute. She refused to go back to college until he was completely healed.

"I'm almost ready." Haley called out from the bathroom. Barrett had let Haley stay in his house and finish out the semester. After finding out who her fiancé really was, Dana had been devastated. She'd really cared for Mark, only to learn he was a psychopath who was going to rape and murder her best friend. Although Dana asked Haley to move back into the dorm with her, Haley said she needed more time. They both did.

"Stop stalling," Jayden called out.

"Who's stalling?" Haley emerged from the bathroom wearing a tight T-shirt, jeans that showed off every curve, and biker boots.

Jayden's mouth went dry as he straightened.

"I'm ready." She propped her hands on her hips and

smirked.

"Let's go then." Jayden opened the front door and let her walk out first.

The summer breeze ruffled her hair and her scent wafted over him, making him hard. Since her stalker had been captured and brought before a Tribunal, they'd not had any time. At the Tribunal, Mark was found guilty and sentenced to death. Jayden was deemed the executioner by Barrett.

She'd not asked how Mark had died. He'd hoped she wouldn't. If she asked, Jayden would tell her. He would tell her they were left alone in a room, where they each shifted into wolf. Mark had attacked first. Jayden let him. He knew once he got a taste of his blood, he wasn't going to stop. He had paid Mark back for all the pain and suffering he'd inflicted on Haley. He'd ripped him apart until you couldn't tell what kind of animal he'd been.

Haley looked at his bike and then back at him. "Are you sure it's okay?"

"Perfectly fine." He handed her a helmet and strapped it on her head.

"I've never been on a Harley before."

"Not just any Harley. A Harley Breakout," Jayden corrected her. She looked gorgeous standing by his bike in those tight jeans. He almost wanted to tell her to forget the whole thing and go back in the house and make love to her.

"I'm ready." She beamed a smile at him.

He straddled his bike and waited for her to settle behind him. She wrapped her arms around his waist and he didn't fight the smile that played at his lips. She felt fucking perfect.

The engine roared to life as he eased onto the street. He accelerated once they turned onto the highway, loving how her body felt against him. He wished they could keep going, keep riding until they ran out of gas. But he knew there was something they had to do.

He turned off the exit and headed in the direction of the university. The semester was over, but summer classes were in full swing, even at this hour of the day.

He slowed his speed as he entered the street that would take him to the center of the college. He stopped and backed into a parking space.

She climbed off and smiled.

"You look incredibly happy for someone who lost a bet." He smirked as he pulled out a couple of towels from his saddlebags.

"Maybe it's my new outlook on life." She smiled as she began taking off her shoes.

"Have you heard from your parents?" He undid the laces on his motorcycle boots and pulled them off.

"I have. They want me to come back home." Jayden's heart stopped in his chest and he looked away. "And what do you want?"

"I told them I am home."

He jerked his gaze to hers.

"I told them that I'm staying here in Arkansas, even after I finish college. I think I'd like to try my clothing line idea."

"I think you'll be a success at it." His heart soared, knowing she wasn't going to leave.

"So are we going to talk or are we going to go for a swim?" She eyed the fountain with interest.

"Come on." He grabbed her hand and tugged her toward the fountain.

They glanced around. No one was out and about and campus security was nowhere in sight.

"We've got to be fast before security shows up." Jayden tugged his shirt over his head. His hands went for his jeans and pulled them down.

Haley nodded and quickly undressed.

His eyes glazed over as she stood ·there without any

clothes on.

"Jayden, come on. We don't' have time for that, not here." She laughed as she pulled him into the fountain.

He hissed as the cold water hit skin. She shivered as she sat down, immersing herself in the water. He did the same. When they came up, there were two college girls gaping.

"Come on. Let's go before we get arrested." Jayden tugged her out of the water.

Laughing, they quickly dried off and threw their clothes back on.

"Hey, you two! Stop!" The campus security guard raced toward them.

Jayden tossed the helmet at Haley as he started the motorcycle. She hopped on behind him.

Ignoring the speed signs, Jayden raced through the campus and out into the road. When they hit the highway, he sped up even further.

Fifteen minutes later they were pulling into a well-known bar. He cut he engine and waited as Haley climbed off.

She gave him a cautious look. "What are we doing here?"

Jayden swallowed and rubbed his sweating palms on his jeans. "I think I owe you a game of pool and maybe a dance." Her eyes widened. "I didn't think you danced."

"I didn't. Not until I met you. It seems there are a lot of things I didn't do until I met you."

Her eyes filled with unspoken emotion. "Oh yeah. Like what kinds of things, Jayden?"

He shoved his hand in his jacket and fumbled for the box.

"For one thing, I'd never fallen in love until I met you." Her lips parted on a silent gasp.

"Haley, I'm in love with you. I've never felt this for another female. Ever. I can't stop thinking about you, even when I'm working. And when I sleep I still dream about you. It's like you have a part of me that I can't get back."

"Your heart?"

"Yeah. You have my heart. You fixed a part of me that I thought was dead. You brought me back to life." He grinned as he took her hand in his.

"I love you too, Jayden."

"Well, thank God for that." He let out a breath.

"Why is that?" She grinned.

"It's going to make this easier." He dropped to one knee and pulled out the little blue box that he'd bought three weeks ago when he'd left the Guardian infirmary.

"Is that what I think it is?" Her eyes widened.

"Haley Guthrie, will you do me the honor of mating me and marrying me?"

"Both?"

"I want you any and every way I can get you. I have found you and I don't ever want to lose you again. I want you bound to me forever. I can't breathe without you, baby."

She fell to her knees and took his face between her hands, kissing him deep. "Yes, Jayden, I will be both your mate and your wife. Forever."

He laughed, feeling freer and happier than he remembered ever feeling before. He pulled the ring from the box and placed the big shiny diamond on her finger.

He stood, pulling her up with him.

"We're not finished."

"There's more?" She grinned as she wrapped her arms around his waist.

He nodded to the bar.

"Are we going to play a game of pool?"

He shook his head. "Not tonight. Tonight I'm taking you dancing."

The End

ABOUT THE AUTHOR

Jodi Vaughn is an USA TODAY Best-selling Southern Paranormal Romance author. When she's not busy playing with her characters and typing away at her laptop, she can be found enjoying a cup of tea (or a very large glass of wine) in her home in Northeast Arkansas. She resides in Arkansas with her family, three dogs, and two fickle swans who travel the neighborhood in search of greener pastures.

Newsletter sign up!

www.ingramcontent.com/pod-product-compliance
Lightning Source LLC
Chambersburg PA
CBHW020750250626
47155CB00003B/1003